HAPPY
Holidates

HAPPY
Holidates

KASEY KENNEDY

Happy Holidates

Copyright © 2025 by Kasey Kennedy

All rights reserved. No part of this publication may be reproduced, stored in a retrieval system, or transmitted in any form or by any means, electronic, mechanical, photocopying, recording, scanning, or otherwise, without the prior written permission except in brief quotations in a book review.

This is a work of fiction. All characters, organizations, and events portrayed in this novel are either products of the author's imagination or are used fictitiously. Any resemblance to persons, living or dead, incidents, and places is coincidental. This is a work of personal creation; no Artificial Intelligence was used in the creation of this manuscript.

ISBN-13: 978-1-958942-24-6 (e-book)

ISBN-13: 978-1-958942-25-3 (paperback)

Cover design by Alt 19 Creative

Author Website:

https://www.kasey-kennedy.com

Published by:

White Eagle Rock Publishing

Other Books by Kasey Kennedy:

IN BLOOM SERIES:
Peonies for Paige
Dahlias for Dominica
Lilies for Lauren
Tulips for Tilly
Wildflowers for Anna Lee

MISTLETOE KISSES SERIES:
Mistletoe for Tricia

SEASIDE BAY SERIES:
Poolside Promises
Beachside Bliss

Other Books:
Love and Pumpkins
Love and Lights (coming Dec. '25)

For my incredible niece,

Kirsten Erlenbusch Billington,

For all our Christmases together—
past, present and future—
my favorite Christmas memories include you.

Chapter One

Renee Magee dreaded walking into her boss's office. She was still reeling with embarrassment from kissing him during Saturday's holiday office party.

What was I thinking?

She blamed it on the mistletoe. *Hello! Who hung the silly decoration right above the punch bowl?*

The sight of the festive greenery had made her forget she was in Chicago, at a corporate event, where she was supposed to be cool, calm, and somewhat collected. But she'd felt a zing of holiday spirit at the sight, which emboldened her to spread a little holiday cheer.

She knew she'd crossed the line during the party. Maybe the punch was extra spiked, or maybe her loneliness got the best of her. Whatever it was, her defenses were down, and when she turned from the punch bowl with a newly filled cup and stared into John's steel-blue eyes, she was a goner. She'd acted on impulse and planted a holiday kiss on his lips.

Her hometown of Minier, in Central Illinois, went all out to celebrate the Christmas holiday, and though she tried to act mature and aloof during the holidays, at her core she was a softie for the colorful lights, gift giving, and taking time to relax.

Every year, as soon as December first rolled around, she developed a hankering for candy canes, hot cocoa, and snickerdoodle cookies. Peppermint, chocolate, and cinnamon. The perfect trifecta of December flavors kept her rolling through the month with a smile on her face and a jingle-jangle in her ears. Of course, the tiny silver bell earrings that she wore almost daily in December helped with the jingle-jangle.

The holidays meant stepping outside of the daily grind and focusing on what was truly important: relationships. From spending extra time with friends and family, to searching for the perfect gifts, to considering her impact on her community and those less fortunate, the end of the year brought Renee a profound sense of charity and belonging that she craved.

She carried a pocketful of one-dollar coins that she ordered each year from the United States Mint to drop into Salvation Army kettles and into the hands of homeless people whenever she could.

She glanced at the cryptic meeting invite again. The name of the meeting was "Quick One on One". Hopefully, he just wanted to clear the air and tell her he would not hold her impulsive action against her. She'd worked for him for two years and had received three promotions in that time. She was excelling on her latest assignment, a large infrastructure project that was critical to the company's objectives. The team was meeting all interim deadlines, and the project was on budget.

She stood and smoothed her navy-blue dress suit. She always wore a suit on the days she was scheduled to present project updates to the executive team.

The nerves flitting through her stomach were due more to the executive presentation than the meeting with John.

The project owner had submitted a new requirement Friday afternoon, and she would have to explain the challenge to the executives. She needed to convince the chief marketing officer to shift his proposed holiday promotion out one week. She had the facts and the figures and had practiced her presentation twenty times on Sunday. John probably just wanted one more review before the executive presentation. She picked up her leather-bound notebook and lucky pen and marched to his office.

Arriving at his partially opened door, Renee could see he was concentrating on his computer screen with his back to her, so she knocked lightly and waited for his response.

"Come in," he said without looking at her. "Shut the door."

His request provoked in her a growing sense of impending doom. It was an open, collaborative company; doors were only closed for bad news.

Sitting in the guest chair, she scooted it close to his desk so she could place her notebook on the corner for any necessary notes. She glanced at her list of talking points for the executive meeting and smiled at John. "Do you want me to go over the messaging for the executive meeting?"

"No," he said. "Have a seat. I'll be just a moment. Finishing an email."

Renee wanted to laugh but held her tongue. John, still focused on his computer monitor, couldn't see that she'd already taken a seat.

While she waited, she glanced around. She'd always found his office bland and sterile. There was a company poster on one wall and an immaculate whiteboard on the other. On his desk sat a pencil cup holding only matching pens and an empty black plastic inbox on one corner. That was it. He bragged that he had a photographic memory, so he needed few notes or reference materials. She'd never tested him per se, but it sure seemed to her that he never forgot a thing.

Shifting her eyes from the boring desk, she looked out the window with its view of murky Lake Michigan and countless skyscrapers in downtown Chicago. She longed for the day when she would have an office with a door and a similar view.

As John typed away, she remembered how dry and cold his lips had felt against hers and the way his eyes had widened in shock afterwards. He'd spluttered for a moment before turning around and walking away. Renee had looked around, thankful for the low lighting and the focus on the dance floor where two people from the engineering department were breakdancing. No one seemed to have noticed the impulsive kiss.

Just another example of her spontaneity getting the best of her.

Resisting the urge to fidget, she ran down her mental to-do list. It was already 10:00 AM, and the list was growing by the minute.

Finally, John turned toward her and sighed. "Renee. I hate to do this, but I'm going to see if I can have you transferred to another team. I've already talked to Melissa, and she would be happy to have you. This may seem abrupt, but what happened Saturday night was over the line. I have a wife and family to consider, and I cannot let rumors knock me off my career trajectory."

The ringing in her ears sounded like cannons firing. It was a twenty-one-gun salute to *her* career.

"I'm sorry." She paused and swallowed. "What did you say about a wife?"

Forget what team she would be on! He couldn't be married! He didn't wear a wedding band. There were no pictures of a family in his office. He'd never even *mentioned* a family, and they'd worked together for a long time! Bile began to bubble and swish in her stomach. Her legs were ready to race to the bathroom if needed.

"I'm married." He spoke slowly, as if he were talking to a child. "My wife's name is Gretchen. We have three kids."

No, no, no! I kissed a married man? Married! Like, married-married! With rings and vows and kids. Gross! I'm going to be sick!

"I...I can't even." Renee gulped. "I've worked with you for years. You've been my boss for years. I have weekly one-on-one meetings with you. How has that never come up before?"

"I keep my personal life separate from my work life."

"Obviously. Hold on." The ringing in her ears would not relent. "Did you say you want me to move to Melissa's team?"

Did I put on deodorant? My pits are damp.

Melissa was a wonderful director, but the optics of moving to another team would be a CLM—career-limiting move.

Renee was grateful he wasn't asking her to resign or firing her outright! She *could* move to another team. It would allow her to maintain her length of service with the company, seniority, and three weeks of paid vacation. It might not be a horrible move; maybe she could spin it the right way and make it positive.

He nodded. "Well, yes. It's either move to her team or resign. If you decide to resign, write a note and email it to me. Then you can go home. You can give a two-week notice, make your last day the fifteenth, but you don't have to come in. I'll take over your project until I can get someone else on it."

"You want me to resign?" The cannon noises in her head morphed into a cacophony of laughter and shouting; she couldn't hear herself think.

Talk about ruining Christmas! What would she tell her family? *Hey, know how I told you how great work was going, and how much I love the company and how respected I am? Well, I threw that all away and quit. At Christmas. With nothing lined up. Merry Christmas!*

John shrugged. "I think you should move to Melissa's team, but it's up to you. You kissed me. It was inappropriate."

"Yes. I agree it was inappropriate! And I shouldn't have done it. I'm sorry. I get overly excited and impulsive during the holidays. But I didn't know you were married!" She nearly choked on that last word.

"Does that really matter?" His eyes seemed to peer into her soul. "I'm your boss."

Renee's head throbbed. How was this her life right now? She'd thrown herself into her career. She was proud of herself for moving to the big city, far from home. Well, three hours was far enough.

How am I going to tell my family? My friends? How am I going to pay my bills? It wasn't cheap living in downtown Chicago.

"But I do a great job..." Should she fight him on this?

"I didn't say otherwise. Melissa knows you'd be an asset to her team." He ran his hand over his military-like buzz cut, the one thing about him she didn't care for. That and the fact that he was married! "It would be untenable for us to keep working together."

Wait. Would John act differently towards me if I moved to Melissa's team? Would he question my decisions? Support me during performance reviews? John and Melissa are peers; it isn't like I'd be moving to a whole new department. Moving to Melissa's team might not be far enough away.

How can my career with this company withstand that kind of setback? There has to be a better position out there. Plus, even if I were on another team, I would still need to interact with John. How can I ever look at this man again?

Her mind flashed back to the most embarrassing moment in her life. At her senior prom, her boyfriend Bryce Rhodes had won the title of prom king, and Alexis Tooley, her toughest competitor in sports and scholastic accolades, had become queen. Renee hadn't been excited about the outcome of the voting, but she'd smiled and congratulated Alexis, anyway.

Bryce stood on the stage, looked at Renee and mouthed, "We're done" as Max Tuel, the prior year's prom king, put the crown on his head.

Everyone understood his meaning. The crowd around Renee started whispering and laughing. Renee's smile froze on her face, and she ran out of the building.

Renee patted herself on the back for appearing cheerful during the last weeks of school. It had been torture watching Bryce and Alexis walking down the hallways arm in arm. Once she'd left for college that fall, she never returned to her hometown for more than a quick visit. She'd found summer jobs and internships that kept her busy and, more importantly, away.

The urge to run again hit her now. Though this time, the urge was—surprisingly—to return home.

Mustering all the dignity that she had left, which was about an ounce, she stood and turned to exit John's office. "I'll have that resignation letter to you this morning, but I'm going to the executive meeting to give my project readout first." She forced her shoulders back to stand confidently in spite of her career careening off the rails. *Fake confidence. You have an executive presentation to give. You can fall apart when you get home.*

"Don't mention this." He waved his hand around, indicating the two of them in his office.

"Of course not." She imagined a magical protective shield going up all around her, felt it clicking into place.

"But I already saw Thomas. He knows I'm here. It would look weird for me to leave now. Wouldn't it?" Thomas was the VP of Technology, and John's boss.

"No." John shrugged again. Renee wanted to punch his shoulder and tell him he looked like a brat doing that. "Not necessarily. It happens all the time."

"Before now, I could never have imagined leaving in the middle of a project. I have a few things to follow up on this morning before the exec meeting. I'll send you an informal status report of open items, next steps and the current project plan. Before I *resign.*"

That word tasted like pine needles on her lips.

Before John could say anything else, she shoved her "lucky" pen into her jacket pocket and exited.

This was the worst day of her career by far. Fa la la, faaaaaaa—.

Chapter Two

Luke Woods stared at the festive elf costume hanging on his office door and groaned. The jacket was green velvet with a wide collar trimmed in red cording and white fur. The matching velvet pants were a little short; he would need tall socks. It came with a green velvet hat shaped like Santa's hat, complete with a large white ball on the end.

He should have asked more questions before agreeing to co-host Minier's Twelve Holly Days of Christmas festival.

He'd signed up to do this with his work buddy Claire. With her by his side, Luke could do anything. But since she'd broken her leg on a skiing trip, chaperoning the high-school ski club in Wisconsin, she could not uphold her end of the bargain.

Claire said she would figure something out. She was a lifetime resident of this small town, whereas he was a one-year transplant. She had better connections than he did.

Moving to Minier was one of life's unexpected detours. He'd been building his business and reputation in Springfield's real estate market when his dad, Michael, had called with three of the most chilling words a son could hear: "I have cancer."

The cancer took a part of Michael's lung and Luke's career goals. He'd had to move to Minier to help his dad out, and though he'd tried to continue working in real estate here, the town wasn't big enough to support another agent. Luckily, he had a counseling degree and accreditation to fall back on. A timely job opening at the high school gave him a needed paycheck, benefits, and rewarding relationships with students and staff.

Luke moved into a small apartment behind his dad's garage. They didn't know the history of why or when it'd been built, but now it seemed fortuitous that his dad had purchased the house with the bonus space years before needing it for Luke. Luke's humble abode was perfect for taking care of his dad—he was close by and could check on his dad frequently, make sure he was eating and taking his medication. The town was growing on him; it was full of kindhearted and quirky people who looked out for each other.

Michael had moved to Minier shortly after Luke graduated from high school. Luke's mom, Lisa, had died from a sepsis infection when Luke was sixteen. The grief drove Michael to change his job and home. He said he couldn't continue to live in the home he'd shared with his wife for so many years. Michael had a good friend who'd lived in Minier when he moved there, though the friend had since moved to Bloomington.

Pulling himself out of his sad memories, Luke shook the costume's green jacket, the tiny bells sewn along the outer edges of the sleeves tinkling. *Well, that's annoyingly cute.*

He knew from attending the planning meetings that he'd be spending a lot of time in the costume over the next couple of weeks. As a festival emcee, he had to attend all the special events that loosely followed "The Twelve Days of Christmas" song. There was a themed activity every night from December twelfth to the twenty-third. On the first day, participants would decorate a Partridge in a Pear Tree card at the library. On the third day, there would be a rubber duck race (they couldn't find rubber French hens) at the fitness center pool.

Luke kept the schedule and descriptions in the back of his planner and referred to the list often.

His office door opened, and Claire shuffled in on her crutches. "Good morning, Hopalong," he greeted.

She huffed out a breath that made her bangs dance. "Wow, this is still challenging, I have to say."

"Nothing better than a PE teacher on crutches. I hope you have an extra whistle."

"Even better," Claire replied, sitting down. She wore a green long-sleeved T-shirt with the Minier Peine High School panther mascot and the girl's track logo. "I have a teacher's aide that can run after the students if needed."

"That's great! How did the administration swing the budget for that?"

"It's my cousin, Paul. He's volunteering until I'm back on my feet."

"There's nothing better than family."

"Speaking of." Claire shifted in her chair, trying to find a comfortable position for her leg. "I have someone to take my place in hosting the Happy Holidates."

Luke smiled at the informal name of the holiday festivities; Claire wasn't the only one who used it. "Not your cousin Paul, I hope." Luke raised an eyebrow. "I'm *not* wearing the female costume."

Claire chuckled. "I'd pay good money to see that, even on my salary. But no, you're off the hook there. My sister Renee is coming home earlier than expected for the holidays, and I sweet-talked her into filling in for me."

"But you've said she hates coming home."

Claire shifted again in the green plastic chair across from Luke's desk. "I know. She usually just comes home on Christmas Eve and leaves on Christmas Day. She's so busy with her city life, there's no time for us small-town folk. But she said she needed to get out of the city for a while. When I talked to her, it didn't sound like she was in the Christmas spirit; she sounded down, even depressed. Anyway, since our parents sold their house before their big trip, she needed a place to crash for a few weeks while she's home, and she begged for my couch. So, she owes me."

"She sounds..." He paused, considering his words, "...awful. Maybe I should try on the lady's costume."

Claire snorted. "Hey, it won't be that bad. At least she's familiar with the Reindeer Games. She'll keep you from making a fool of yourself."

"Based on what little you've said about her, I'm not so confident." Luke took a sip of his coffee and reached for a scone.

Claire shook her head. "I'm sorry, I shouldn't have put her in such a negative light. There are a ton of great things about her. She's a go-getter. If there's a problem, she'll work night and day to fix it. She's funny, outgoing, and adventurous. Actually..." Claire smiled at him with her mischievous grin. "You two might be perfect for each other. You've been saying you'd like to find someone. Maybe your someone will be in an elf costume. You'll have plenty of opportunities to get to know her."

"Wouldn't it be weird for me to date your sister?"

"As long as you two don't put me in the middle and have me relaying messages or interpreting why someone said something, it'll be fine. I'm Switzerland."

"Noted. What about your dating life? Maybe we should each make a New Year's goal to date more."

Claire scoffed. "I'm still reeling from my last breakup. I'm perfectly happy being single."

"There's nothing wrong with that. What's your sister's story?"

He glanced at the time on his phone—thirty minutes until the first class. They typically walked to the cafeteria for coffee and a bagel before classes started, but since she'd broken her leg, he'd brought breakfast and had it ready when she arrived.

He was happy to have an excuse to bake muffins, scones, and croissants. When pressed, he told Claire that he was driving to Morton and buying from a bakery there. That was a whopper of an untruth. He shared a lot with Claire but hadn't shared his baking passion.

Claire grabbed an apple off his desk and peeled the sticker off it. "Did you wash these?"

"Of course."

"Cool. Well, Renee is Renee, a typical attention-grabbing middle sibling. She's always had big plans and bigger dreams. She was making plans to get out of Minier from the age of seven. Never wanted to live in a small town, wanted more than this town could offer her. There was a time in high school when I thought she would change her mind and stay. She fell in love with the senior quarterback. High-school hero. She started talking about getting married and having babies. Things were great until they weren't."

"Ah. A broken heart." Luke witnessed a lot of broken hearts while counseling students; he stored a dozen boxes of tissues in his office to console them. "That's too bad. Is she involved with anyone now?"

"I'm not sure. She doesn't share much. Just talks about work and the fun things she's doing. Museums, plays, culture." Claire rolled her eyes with a smile.

"So, you're the athletic one and she's the sophisticated one. And your brother is the handy goofball. Got it."

"Something like that." Claire finished the apple and dropped the core into his wastebasket. "I'd like to say we're each more well-rounded than that, but you may be right. Anyway. You'll get to meet her this week. She's coming in tomorrow and staying until Christmas."

"Wow! Christmas is still three weeks away. She has that much time off?"

"I didn't think so. She was vague about why she's coming early. Maybe she can work remotely. Who knows? Well." Claire looked at her watch. "I should hobble on down to the gym. The first-period bell will ring soon, and

I need to have a word with Paul before the day gets out of hand. See you at lunch?"

"Wouldn't miss it."

Luke watched her pick up a cranberry scone, wrap it in a napkin, and shove it into her backpack. She eased out of the chair and navigated an about-face on her crutches, making her way through the utilitarian hallway that housed the teacher's lounge and several offices. He hated seeing his friend in pain. Claire was tough, but not immune to broken bones, and was feeling frustrated at her current situation.

As Claire exited his office, Luke looked at the day's schedule, filled with appointments with eight seniors to discuss post-high school options. He'd spent the evening before preparing for each meeting. Thinking about Claire's comments regarding her sister, he wasn't sure what he was getting himself into with this holiday festivities emcee gig, and he hoped his partner would make it easier, not harder. Time would tell.

Chapter Three

Renee pulled a black sweater out of her suitcase, which was currently taking up the corner of her sister's living room. The corner Claire wanted to put her Christmas tree in this weekend, as she'd reminded Renee three times already. Renee needed to find a new home for her suitcase.

Grabbing a pair of black slacks, she dashed to the bathroom to change. With her sister being out of commission, there was a lot she needed to do this morning before attending a meeting with the festival committee.

The committee was meeting in the afternoon before the opening ceremony of what the locals lovingly called "Reindeer Games", and the town officially called the "Twelve Holly Days of Christmas". Before then, Renee needed to run around town, hang up fliers, pick up donated supplies, and stop in to review the evening's agenda with Mayor Malloy. He would be the one to light the tree when the time came, and though he'd done it forty-seven times before, Claire had stressed the fact that the mayor needed a few reminders.

It had been years since Renee had attended the event. Eleven years, but who was counting? She normally came home just in time for Christmas Eve dinner at her parents' house, and luckily for her, the festival was over by then. She avoided town-focused activities, worried she would run into her high school ex-boyfriend—heavy emphasis on the ex. Or her high school nemesis, the one who stole said ex on prom night.

Renee reached for the flatiron and grabbed the wrong end. "YE-OW!" she screeched, hoping she didn't wake Claire. It wasn't even 6:00 AM, but she was used to getting up early, and she had a lot to do today. As soon as she checked off all the festival tasks, she would update her resumé and compile a list of companies that interested her. *Figures, just thinking about Bryce and Alexis causes pain. I should have known.*

She finished getting ready, filled a coffee cup with dark roast, and grabbed the stack of fliers she needed to plaster around town. She tried to remember why Claire's partner hadn't done this task once Claire broke her leg. It seemed like Claire had mentioned it, but Renee couldn't remember. Her mind was stuck on a loop, replaying the mortification of kissing John at the work holiday party and her decision to quit abruptly.

Quitting wasn't the wisest decision. She wasn't sure how she was going to afford her apartment without her income. She sighed. *I can't think about that right now. I've volunteered to cover for Claire, and I'm going to execute with precision and grace.*

Climbing into her Mini Cooper, she affixed her to-do list to the dashboard, using the roll of Washi tape she kept in the glovebox for that purpose. She glanced over the list one more time and put the car in gear. First stop, the Filling Station on Main Street.

Parking a few minutes later, she reached over and grabbed the poster and a stack of handouts to leave with Gary, the owner. Though she avoided big events when she was home, she always stopped to see Gary while she was in town. Working at the breakfast and lunch counter at the Filling Station had been her favorite job in high school.

The Filling Station was a one-stop shop for farmers and townspeople alike. You could fill up your gas tank, fill up your stomach, and fill up on the local news, and gossip, all before eight in the morning.

Renee opened the door and grinned as the rich smells—bacon, coffee, and hash browns—hit her. Three of the basic food groups in this part of the state.

Gary glanced up from behind the register and whooped a hello before coming out to give her a hug. "Whelp, who do we got here? Heard you were in town and hoped to get to see you. How long are you home for?"

"A couple of weeks, at least." Renee held up the stack of fliers, and Gary gestured to a corner of the counter where she dropped them. "I'm filling in for Claire for the Reindeer Games."

"The big bosses let you off work for that long, huh?" He grinned.

"I'm actually between roles right now, so it was perfect timing."

There. Truthful, but not too forthcoming. She was thankful no one here would ever know about her work humiliation. Seemed no one ever forgot about her 'dumped on prom night' debacle. Almost every time she came home, someone mentioned it at least once.

"Lucky news for the town, then. Grab yourself some breakfast. Grinch eggs are on special today."

"Sorry, no time. But I will grab a Danish to go." Gary's cook, Alice, made the best homemade Danishes; Renee had woken up from a dream about them that morning.

"Suit yourself." Gary took his spot behind the register and greeted a farmer who was entering.

Renee darted between the two aisles offering everything from toilet paper and bread to shampoo and air filters. Gary carried everything someone had asked him for in the last two years. He took copious notes and aimed to please.

The dining counter, with its eight stools, lined the west side of the building. Of course, someone occupied every seat. Gary's was a popular place.

Renee made her way to the end where the food pickup sign hung. She took a quick glance at the people sitting at the counter. From the backs of their heads, she didn't recognize anyone. She hoped no one would turn around and recognize her. She had too many stops to make before her meeting with the mayor at eleven.

Approaching the small space to make a go order, she smiled to see the man on the last stool. He was wearing a Santa hat with a bell on the end that jingled softly as he shifted.

Renee was about to comment on the festive hat when Alexis Tooley-Owens walked out of the kitchen carrying two plates in one hand and a coffee pot in the other.

Renee groaned softly, which caught the attention of the stranger in the Santa hat.

He tilted his head slightly and glanced at her with a side-eye. "Is the hat that bad?" he asked.

Whoa! Who is this hunky man? Dark brown hair covered his jawline. Normally, she didn't like facial hair on a man — too itchy when kissing — but thoughts of his scruff on her skin sent a shiver down her spine.

Maybe kissing someone new would help erase the mortification of kissing her boss and finding out he was married. Sure, sure, she should never have kissed her boss to begin with—obvious in hindsight.

"Oh, your hat is fine..."

"Get out!" Alexis shouted, seeing Renee. "Is it really you, Miss Magoo?"

Renee's cheeks flushed. The childhood nickname still produced a visceral reaction. There was no flight, only fight.

Everyone sitting at the counter turned towards her. There were a couple of "heys" and a soft "howdy" from the men and two women perched on the stools.

"Hi, Alexis. How've you been?" Renee asked, rising above her discomfort.

"Great! What are you doing home so early? I thought you were a reindeer that rode in on Christmas Eve and flew out on Christmas Day?" Alexis laughed at her own joke.

Alexis, her arch-nemesis in high school, was smart, talented and a knockout. They were always competing, whether it was in track, on the stage, in a speech competition, running for class president—you name it.

Her heart raced as she remembered that awful prom night when Alexis won the queen title and stole Bryce. The night Renee vowed to leave Minier and never set foot in it again for longer than absolutely necessary. Hence, the reindeer in and out comment from Alexis.

Lifting her right heel, which was a power habit she used whenever she needed to shore up her resolve and/or go into battle, Renee smiled brightly. "I earned some extra time off for the holidays, so I'm home early."

Okay, some could interpret that as a lie, but she was going with it.

"That's great! You deserve it. Gotta put these plates down, be right with you!" Alexis's voice was so warm and cheerful, it made Renee want to like her.

That's not likely to happen.

Alexis slid a plate in front of the man in the Santa hat and gave him a wink and a shoulder shrug. *Flirt.*

So much for a Danish. Renee was not standing around waiting to be helped by Alexis. She turned on her heel and left, telling Gary she'd be back soon. *Just not today.*

Chapter Four

Luke parked his car and leaned over to grab the cranberry orange cheesecake he'd made the night before. He exited the car and started the trek up the long flight of stairs to Claire's apartment.

Claire lived above the beauty shop in downtown Minier. Thankfully, that meant a short two-block walk to the tree-lighting ceremony after dinner. He knew Claire was having a hard time getting up and down the stairs on her crutches. She had asked her brother Caleb to make small platforms for the bottom of the crutches to keep them from getting stuck in the cracks of the open metal steps, but they weren't ready yet. The open pattern helped keep snow or water from puddling or stacking up on the stairs, but it was no good for crutches.

Knocking on the door, he glanced down at the parking lot and noticed a bright red Mini Cooper. He wondered if it belonged to Claire's sister, whom he was here to meet.

The door opened, and he nearly took a step back. Somehow, as he speculated about Claire's "little sister," he never imagined the beautiful woman in front of him.

Claire was athletic and friendly, while this woman was slender to a fault and looked like she'd rather stab someone than be their friend.

"You must be Renee." He shifted the cake to his left hand and stuck out his right.

"I must be. You're Luke." She squinted at him; her eyes searching his intently. A flash of guilt zipped through him, like he'd been busted taking the last cookie. When she placed her hand in his to shake, he almost dropped the dessert dish.

"I am." He nodded. "Pleasure to meet you. Looking forward to hosting the festivities with you."

She rolled her eyes and pulled the door wider. "Come in. Claire's at the kitchen table. I have to—never mind."

Renee walked towards the corner of Claire's soothing beige living room with its comfy couch and minimal decorations. She began shuffling through a suitcase sitting on the floor, and Luke turned away when a pink bra fell out.

He walked into the kitchen and greeted Claire. "Don't get up. What can I do to help?" he asked, glancing at the stove where a large pot of yummy, earthy-smelling soup was simmering.

"Nothing." Claire began stacking a pile of papers on the table. It looked as if she were grading papers. "We've got it under control. When the timer goes off, I'll have you grab the rolls out of the oven. We'll be ready to eat soon."

"Smells delicious." He set the cheesecake on the counter and shrugged out of his jacket. "I brought dessert, as promised."

"Wonderful. You can toss your jacket on the back of the couch," Claire said. "Well, are you ready to be indoctrinated into the Reindeer Games?"

"Ready as I can be." Luke smiled, his eyes wide. "I'm sorry you're not able to do this with me. I think we would have had a great time."

Renee walked past him and shot him a look. "We'll have fun."

"Right. Of course, hey, were you at Gary's this morning? Your voice sounds familiar." He remembered Alexis's loud greeting and the woman who'd approached the counter but left before getting anything.

She tilted her head; her interrogating eyes locked on his face. "Were you the guy in the Santa hat sitting at the counter?"

"Guilty."

Her skin was pale, so it was easy to see her cheeks flush, and Luke thought it was the cutest thing. He tried to remember the gist of the conversation between her and Alexis this morning. They'd bantered for a minute before Alexis put his plate down.

Renee shifted. "There's no better place to eat breakfast in town."

Claire laughed. "There's nowhere else to get breakfast, sis."

"Why didn't you?" Luke asked.

"Why didn't I what?"

"Get breakfast?"

"Oh, I...realized I was late. Had to dash."

Claire's head was bouncing between the two of them, like she was watching a tennis match. "What could you possibly be late for? You were just dropping off fliers this morning."

Renee shot her sister a look, and Luke decided it was best to change the subject. He was about to discuss the tree-lighting ceremony when the timer went off.

"I'll grab that," he said, spinning around to look for an oven mitt. Finding a mitt with a chihuahua face on it—he'd have to ask Claire what that was about later—he opened the oven and pulled out the baking sheet with the rolls.

He placed the sheet on an empty burner and stirred the soup while he was there. "Wow, this soup looks amazing! What is it?"

"It's stone soup," both sisters said at once.

Luke turned slowly and looked from one to the other. "Excuse me. Did you say stone soup?"

Claire smiled, and Renee rolled her eyes. Again. That seemed to be a habit of hers.

"Am I going to break a tooth if I eat it?" he asked when neither woman answered.

"No," Claire laughed. "No stones were harmed or used in making the soup."

Luke leaned against the counter. "Then, why the name?"

Renee stepped up to the stove and gave the soup a stir. She pointed at a basket lined with a towel on the counter, indicating it was for the rolls. "It's a term our Grandma Louise used. She said it came from the hobo days. There was a story of a hobo coming to a home and asking if he could make a 'magical' stone soup."

Luke used tongs to move the rolls to the basket. "He had a stone?"

"Yes, of course." Renee stopped stirring and glanced at her sister. "He came into the woman's house…"

"Whose house?" Luke asked.

"Let's just say our Grandma Louise's house, but it was unclear if this ever really happened to her," Renee said. "Anyway, he asked to make stone soup, and she let him in. He then got a pot of water, put his stone in it, and then asked if Grandma had any carrots. Then he asked her for every vegetable or piece of meat known to man, per Grandma, until there was a wonderful dump-in vegetable beef soup cooking on the stove."

"Ah, a trick, so he could eat."

"One could look at it that way," Claire said. "But we prefer to think of it as a blessing, not a trick."

"Wow!" Luke nodded. "And your grandma lived to tell the tale. So, it was all good in the end."

"Sure. And we learned how to make a beef veggie dump soup, AKA stone soup." Renee took a spoon out of the drawer and tasted the soup. "It's ready. I'll get the bowls and dish up. Would you mind putting the rolls on the table?"

As they sat and ate, Luke pumped the sisters for information. "So, tell me what to expect tonight? Why aren't we required to be elves for this evening's festivities? Doesn't the tree lighting kick off the Twelve Holidates?"

Renee slathered her roll with butter. Luke wondered how she stayed so slim. She was probably a workout nut like Claire.

Claire leaned forward. "The mayor likes to be in the spotlight at the tree lighting. I think he worries the elves will upstage him."

Luke nodded. "I haven't had a lot of interaction with him at the planning meetings, but I can see what you're saying. He likes things the way he likes them."

"Yes, which keeps this town in the 1950s," Renee said, vehemently. "He's been the mayor for a hundred years and refuses to listen to new ideas. And he absolutely hates the idea of progress."

"Hey, that's harsh coming from someone who doesn't live here," Claire admonished. "Mayor Malloy is good for this town."

"I heard a rumor that he may be retiring?" Luke said.

"What?" Renee squeaked.

"Really?" Claire asked.

"Yes, it came up in Tuesday's planning meeting. I heard Alexis tell Mrs. Byrd."

"How would she know?" Renee asked.

"She's his niece. Remember?" Claire answered.

"Oh, I didn't know that." Luke reached for another roll.

"Surprised she didn't mention it in every meeting," Renee said, glancing at her sister. "Seems like something she'd do."

"Drop it, NeyNey."

"NeyNey?" Luke smiled. "I like it."

Renee's eyes looked murderous. "My sister is the only one allowed to call me that."

Luke raised his hands. "Duly noted."

Claire's sister intrigued him. He asked questions about life in Chicago and her job. Renee answered the questions succinctly, and Claire chimed in only a few times, not to tease but to support.

Claire, who never let him off the hook, who teased everyone ruthlessly, seemed like she was the younger sister, used to deferring to Renee. This side of Claire was shocking. Confusing. Claire always spoke highly of her sister. He knew she was proud of the things she had achieved professionally, but she rarely talked about what kind of person Renee was. What did she do for fun? What made her laugh?

Renee would answer a direct question, but she didn't overshare. She reminded him of some of the hardest students to crack. She appeared well-put together and poised on the outside, but she was likely dealing with a lot underneath.

Like sees like. I've kept that joyful, outwardly happy persona myself for years. I see you, Renee Magee, and I've cracked tougher nuts than you.

Once they finished eating dinner, Luke offered to clean up. They all agreed to wait for dessert until after they got home, to give their stomachs time to digest dinner. Renee looked relieved and said she wanted to freshen up before they left for the tree lighting, and Claire appreciated being able to keep her broken leg propped up a little longer.

Luke hummed as he cleared the table and started running water in the sink to wash the dishes.

"What are you humming?" Claire asked.

"I don't know. I think the school band was playing it as I left today. Catchy little ditty."

"They're performing tonight." Claire shifted in her seat. "Maybe we'll hear it again."

Luke didn't know that the Minier Peine High School band was performing tonight. Since this was his first

Christmas holiday in Minier and his services weren't required for the tree lighting tonight, he wasn't clued in on the details. He was glad it was going to be a surprise.

Kind of like Renee. He'd expected a mini-Claire, but she was definitely her own person. He liked what he'd seen so far. She might be a little restless and way too serious, but he thought they'd make great co-hosts for the coming festivities. He hoped so anyway. He needed something to distract himself from his dad's poor health and bad moods. Things had seemed to improve lately, but it was hard to stay positive when his dad had so many bad days.

He took a deep breath as he plunged his hands into the hot, soapy water. He'd asked Claire what to expect during the evening's program, but his mind kept jumping between the color of Renee's eyes and the list of tasks he needed to complete for his dad over the weekend. At least the first day of Christmas festivities wasn't until Tuesday night. He hoped to get things settled with his dad before then so he could give the twelve days his all.

Chapter Five

After helping Claire navigate to a bench alongside the library, where she had a great view of the Christmas tree that was set up in the middle of the intersection at Main and Peoria, Renee and Luke purchased cups of hot cocoa from a street vendor whose mobile coffee van was decorated to look like Santa's sleigh, complete with a real, live reindeer tied to the front. A woman helped facilitate pictures with the reindeer—for kids only, Luke was disappointed to discover. They took a cup of chocolatey goodness to Claire, then joined the throng of people gathered around the tree to wait for the lighting ceremony.

When the original founders of the town designed the downtown street, they created a roundabout in this intersection. Peoria Street ran north and south, and Main Street east and west. Both roads led in and out of town from their respective directions. Renee always wondered if the original vision for this spot had included the plans for a twenty-five-foot evergreen tree.

Luke's conversation with a teenager standing in front of them interrupted Renee's musing about the age of the tree that had been cut down to be put on display for only a month.

Luke had tapped the kid on the shoulder.

"Hey, Mr. Woods," the young man said, turning towards them.

"How are you, James?" Luke asked in an upbeat voice. "You missed your appointment with me yesterday."

The kid looked down. "Sorry 'bout that. Flu bug."

"Ah, yuck." Luke said. "Well, it's great that you're feeling well enough to be out here. Take care of yourself. Let's reschedule that meeting soon."

"Okay." James nodded, then turned around.

Luke turned to Renee. "So, what do you look forward to the most during the holidays?"

Renee took a sip of her cocoa before answering. This guy was talkative. "Christmas Eve. We go to a late church service and then we stay up really late watching Christmas movies, eating junk food, and talking." She sighed. "But that's changing. Our parents sold their house and are going on a six-month cruise in January. I don't know what they plan to do after that. They may retire in South Carolina. Claire and Caleb seem to be rooted here, so I don't know what our holidays will look like after this year."

"And you're rooted in Chicago?"

She glanced up. The fire ladder cart, which held the mayor and fire chief, was moving. The cart would lift them to the top of the tree, where they would "light" the topper and the rest of the lights would illuminate.

"For now, I am," she replied. "But I'm sending out resumés and am open to moving for the right opportunity."

She didn't want to tell him she was about as rooted in Chicago as a dandelion seed. Her lease was up on February first, and she couldn't afford to stay where she was with no income. If she could land a job by mid-January, she *might* be able to keep her apartment.

Sleeping on Claire's couch would be fine through Christmas, but she didn't want it to turn into a long-term solution.

Times like this reminded Renee that she really, really needed to figure out the whole savings thing. But maintaining her lifestyle—weekly mani/pedis, champagne brunches every weekend, treating friends and coworkers to Thursday nights out, and shopping—was expensive. There was never enough left over to save.

She had been doing so well at her job; she predicted she was on the fast path to a director's role in another year or two, then she would have the salary to save for a rainy day. She was not prepared for the downpour that came after quitting abruptly.

"Right opportunity? What are you looking for, exactly?" Luke's eyes trailed up the tree, and he leaned toward her to hear her response.

"Another project management position at a company that offers room for advancement." She'd repeated this mantra so many times in her head that the words sounded robotic and dull.

The crowd started cheering, and it was hard to hear over the noise, but Luke leaned even closer to ask, "Why is advancement so important to you?"

The smell of his aftershave overpowered the sweet chocolate and peppermint scent rising from the cocoa.

Renee paused to hyper-focus on the earthy, comforting notes of his cologne. Luke was the best-smelling high school counselor she'd ever met, albeit, the second one she'd ever met. She couldn't even remember the name of her high school counselor at the moment. Closing her eyes, she realized that Luke's deep green eyes had left an impression as well, as they were the only thing she could picture with her eyes closed.

"I want to win," she answered. Surely, he would understand the competitiveness that ran in her family. Being the middle child with super-athletic Claire and highly intelligent Caleb made a person competitive. She couldn't beat her siblings in athletic or scholastic ability, so she had to beat them every other way possible. Internally, she carried her own self-declared badges for neatest, first to finish, boldest, most outgoing, funniest, and most ambitious daughter.

"And how do you know you're winning in the corporate world?" he asked.

Renee realized he'd put his hand on her lower back, probably to prevent himself from falling over on her as he leaned down. He was a good five inches taller, she noted.

She rattled off her definition of work success. "Yearly promotions, yearly raises, special awards, number of direct reports, being assigned the most prestigious projects. There are lots of ways."

Luke nodded and straightened. The streetlights were suddenly extinguished, and the mayor's voice started booming over the loudspeakers set around the square. "Ladies and gentlemen. We are excited that you've been able to gather here this evening to help us kick off the holiday season with the lighting of the tree. As mayor, I have the duty and honor of lighting the tree, under the watchful eye of our Fire Chief, Chief Brandt."

The mayor took a deep breath, and Renee rolled her eyes, thankful that Luke couldn't see her.

"This tree-lighting ceremony has been running for sixty-four years, ever since a small group of energetic citizens set about bringing the magic of the holiday spirit to town. Lucky for us, a band of revelers has continued the tradition ever since. I would like to thank the Spirit Committee for another season of fun, engaging activities. The Twelve Holly Days of Minier's Christmas will kick off on Tuesday at the library. Join Santa's elves as they lead us in decorating holiday cards. And, as always, have a holly, jolly, good time!"

Luke looked at Renee and smiled broadly, lifting his eyebrows quickly. "That's us," his look seemed to say.

Renee was not looking forward to twelve nights of putting on fake smiles and acting cheerful among little kids with runny noses and frazzled parents eager to dump their wired kiddos into the hands of free babysitters.

But at least Luke would be there. She'd only known him for a couple of hours, but she could see why Claire liked him. He was curious, a great listener, and kind. He always seemed to be smiling, and everyone who had greeted him seemed genuinely happy to see him. Luke could be the joyful elf, and she would be the bossy elf. They'd balance each other out.

The mayor's voice boomed. "Let the countdown begin! Ten! Nine!"

The townspeople joined in. Renee took a sip of cocoa. There were worse ways she could spend her time between jobs. At least the twelve days of celebratory activities were at night, and she would have all day to job hunt, send resumés, and hopefully have a few online interviews.

Time with her family over the holidays would be a bonus. This would be the last holiday like the ones she'd grown up with. It was time for new traditions. She was going to take advantage of the time she had at home with her family. By this time next year, there was no telling where they would be.

She reminded herself that as handsome and nice as Luke seemed, she was not here to fall in love with a small-town guy. She had dreams and goals that did not include moving home and settling down.

When she dreamed of falling in love and settling down, she imagined it would be with a professional, an executive in the C-suite, not a high-school guidance counselor. No way was that happening.

After the ceremony, Renee and Luke met Claire at the bench. She was having a conversation with a parent of one of her volleyball players. It was easy to tell, as the daughter was standing beside her mom, wearing a Minier Peine H.S. Volleyball letterman's jacket.

Renee remembered how envious she had been of her siblings' letterman jackets in high school. Claire and Caleb were both athletic, while Renee excelled on the speech and debate team, student council, and theater. Activities that she knew would help her get into college and secure a job once she was out.

Still, no one threw a ticker-tape parade for the speech team, but they sure did for the sports teams. All of them. Claire led the team to the state championships in volleyball and basketball. Caleb was on the football and track teams that brought home state trophies. Those teams were highlighted on the giant "Home Of" sign as you drove into town, but the winning debate team was not.

Luke joined in the conversation quickly, recognizing the mother and daughter talking to Claire. Renee shuffled her cold feet and wished she had put on snow boots. In her hurry to pack and get out of Chicago, she'd forgotten to bring the brand-new sherpa-lined boots she'd found in a cute boutique in Lincoln Park. Now, thinking about the two hundred and fifty dollars she'd spent on them, she sort of wished she could return them. Or wear them. It didn't matter; she couldn't do either right now.

In a futile effort to warm her feet, she walked down the sidewalk a few paces. She noticed that the old movie theater, which had closed in the seventies, was boarded up. Looking closer, she noticed black soot on the building. She ducked down the alleyway and upon closer inspection, she saw that the back-half of the building had collapsed, obviously from a fire.

Wonder when this happened. I don't remember it being like this the last time I was home.

Someone should do something about this. It's an eyesore. And perhaps even a hazard. Kids could climb up the fire escape and break in through the second-story window. Ask Renee how she knew.

"Hey, hey!" Luke's voice called out, and she jumped. "Claire's ready to go. Will you help me walk her back?"

"Sure. I'm ready to get inside myself."

Once they'd navigated the metal stairway and returned to Claire's apartment, Claire declared it was time for dessert.

"I'll put on a pot of coffee. Do you want regular or decaf?" Claire asked.

"Regular for me," Renee answered.

"Same. After that hot cocoa, I'm going to be wired for a while, anyway. I can stay up and work on grading papers."

"I thought you were just a counselor," Renee said, grabbing the creamer from the refrigerator.

"I'm not sure any counselor is *just* a counselor. But I also teach one of the American history classes. This year's freshman class was twenty-five percent larger than last year's, and they needed some teaching help."

Claire clicked the coffeepot on and hopped over to the table, where she lowered herself with a sigh. "Good thing Luke could cover that class; you know I hate teaching history."

Renee laughed. "I'm properly chagrined about saying just a counselor, Luke. I didn't mean to offend. It was a poor choice of words. Did you always want to teach and counsel?"

"Well, my career has meandered. I was a good student and enjoyed school, so I got a degree in education and counseling, and I did that for a year out of college. But then I got interested in real estate, got my license and I was building a decent business in Springfield, where I'm from, before my dad got sick. He's got cancer. I moved here in January to help take care of him, and luckily the school needed a counselor. I don't know if you know, but Lucinda Green has the real-estate market here locked up."

"Oh, we know," Renee answered, looking at Claire. "She's best friends with our mom."

"Gotcha. I've met her; she's nice. But there's not enough business here to support two agents."

"What will happen when your dad gets better? Will you move back to Springfield?"

Springfield was way bigger than Minier, but still a small city.

Luke smiled, and Renee noticed how the corners of his eyes crinkled. "First, I appreciate that you said 'when' and not 'if,' and I don't know. I'm enjoying it here. There's something special about the small-town atmosphere. People are quick to help, and everyone looks out for one another. It's nice."

"Everyone is looking *at* one another," Renee said, "but I'm not convinced they're looking out for one another. I find the familiarity stifling."

The coffeepot finished its gurgling, and the room fell silent. Renee replayed her comment in her head and realized how harsh it sounded. She sounded like a stuck-up brat who hated her hometown. That wasn't completely true. A prickly tingle shot along her shoulders.

"What I mean is," she began, but was interrupted by her sister.

"Which of you is cutting the cheesecake?" Claire asked. "I'm ready for something sweet."

Unlike my sour remark, Renee surmised. "I will," she answered, reaching for a cutting knife hanging on the magnetic rack beside the coffeepot.

Claire's kitchen was small but efficient. Claire wasn't into a lot of frills. She was a minimalist. She'd told Renee that after the fast pace of teaching and coaching, she liked to come home and unwind. Soft pastel colors, clean lines, and an organized space helped her do just that.

Luke retrieved the cheesecake from the fridge and pulled the lid off the container.

"I thought you bought your desserts at a bakery," Claire said. "Why is it in a plastic container?"

Luke looked embarrassed for a second. Renee wondered if a female friend had made it for him to bring.

"I made this one." He shrugged. "Cheesecake is pretty easy to whip together."

Renee couldn't imagine that cheesecake was easy. Nothing she'd ever baked, or cooked for that matter, had been easy. They were all pretty ridiculous, not pretty easy.

"What? A man of many talents!" Claire exclaimed. Renee studied her sister. Was she flirting with Luke? Did she like Luke? She was going to grill her sister after this guy took off.

I wonder if we can get him to leave the cheesecake; it looks amazing.

The cheesecake had very faint specks of orange peel in the mix. On top of the cake were candied cranberries, sparkling with specks of sugar, arranged in a snowflake pattern. The edges held perfectly placed dollops of whipped topping.

"Oh, it looks luscious!" Renee exclaimed, leaning closer to inspect the sugared cranberries. As she got closer, the sweet smells of cranberry, orange, and a hint of cinnamon wafted towards her. She closed her eyes and inhaled. "I can't wait to taste it!"

"You've got the knife; you're holding up progress!" Claire laughed.

"Yes, ma'am. I'm on it."

She cut each of them a generous slice.

"I can't believe you made this," Claire said, taking a bite. She closed her eyes and sighed loudly.

Renee quickly took a bite herself and groaned; it was delicious.

"You're leaving this here, right?" she asked Luke. "Don't forget, my sister is injured. She's a helpless shut-in this weekend. With the snow and the paper-grading, there's no way she's going to leave her apartment all weekend. We'll, I mean, *she'll* need provisions. Sugar is provision-providing!" Renee said.

Luke dropped his head backwards and laughed, a long, loud laugh, filled with glee and mirth. *Santa's helper on steroids.* Renee grinned at the thought. Slowly, she felt her own joy bubble up. At least partnering with Luke in co-hosting the Christmas festivities would not be as painful as she had feared.

Chapter Six

When Claire suggested putting up a Christmas tree after church on Sunday, Renee was all for it, and she talked their brother Caleb into cutting down a live tree from his farm instead of getting Claire's artificial tree out of storage. Renee was looking forward to sleeping in the same room as a pine tree for the next few weeks. Falling asleep and waking up to an evergreen smell sounded like the cheering up she needed.

Luke was coming over and had promised something sweet, warm, and yummy, so Renee skipped breakfast. She regretted her decision at eleven-thirty when her stomach did a back-spring somersault.

Claire laughed. "I heard that. Told you to eat eggs this morning."

"They weren't eggs," Renee protested, "they were egg *whites*. Yuck."

"Still, it was substance, and now you're hungry. It's your own fault."

"You never fail to point out my faults, do you, sis?"

"It's sort of my job."

Renee laughed. They'd had this exact conversation many, many times over the years. "When is your buddy getting here?"

The sisters were stringing popcorn to hang on the Christmas tree. A speaker connected to Claire's phone was playing Christmas music, and it was snowing outside. The perfect day for putting up a tree. They were waiting for Caleb to bring the tree, and Luke was coming to help their brother wrangle it up the stairs.

"He said he'd be here by one. Patience. Maybe you should eat a sandwich while we're waiting."

Renee glanced at her watch. It was a few minutes before the hour. She could wait. "What else do you need help with while I'm here? Anything I can do this week while you're at school? Need me to shop? Run errands?"

Claire's eyes sparkled. "Serious? If you could help with my Christmas shopping, I would be indebted."

"You're already indebted. I'm handling your elfin responsibilities."

"True. But I'll be even more indebted."

"Make a list." Renee pushed a piece of popcorn onto the needle and pulled it down the string. This was tedious. "Happy to help. Besides, I need to keep busy. I'm not used to having all this time on my hands."

"Right. Do you regret quitting your job?"

In a moment of frustration, Renee had confessed to her sister the reason for quitting her job and coming home early for the holidays. Taking a deep breath, she said, "I don't want to talk about it. It's in the past. It's time to move forward. I'm sure I'll find something bigger and better, but job hunting right before Christmas is the worst. I can't imagine anyone responding until January, after the holidays."

There was a knock on the door. "I'll get it." Renee stood, thankful to take a break from stringing popcorn.

She opened the apartment door to find Luke holding two large brown boxes. "Hello," he said.

Renee wondered what he'd brought, and she wanted to grab the boxes out of his hands. "Hi. Come in. We're in the kitchen, stringing popcorn."

She gestured for him to precede her, and she tried to get a whiff of the goodies he was carrying. But his cologne drew her attention. It was a light, fresh scent that reminded her of the beach. A nice juxtaposition to gingerbread, popcorn, and the cinnamon candle burning on the kitchen counter.

Following closely, she admired the way he moved. Confident and casual, he was a person who was comfortable in his own skin. Good-looking men usually were.

Good-looking? Well, yeah. He is. Not a crime to notice, I guess.

Luke set the bakery boxes on the counter and unzipped his jacket as he commented on the popcorn-string assembly line on the kitchen table.

Claire shrugged. "I needed something to keep me busy. I'm going stir-crazy."

"Right," Luke said. "But you need downtime to heal. What time will your brother be here?"

"Soon. Renee, will you take Luke's coat and hang it in the closet?"

"Absolutely."

She wanted to just toss the coat on a chair so she could grab whatever he'd brought to eat.

Back in the kitchen, Luke opened a cabinet door to get out plates, and Renee peeked into the box. *Muffins! Yes!*

"These look amazing! I'm glad I didn't eat lunch," Renee said.

"Or breakfast," Claire added.

"You must be hungry." Luke handed Renee a plate. "Dig in."

"These smell like heaven. Where did you get them?" Renee selected a lemon poppyseed muffin, her favorite.

"An old-fashioned family bakery in Morton."

"I need the address," Renee said. She sat down at the table, pushed the popcorn bowl away, and grabbed a red and green plaid cloth napkin. Claire hated paper napkins.

"Sure. I'll get it for you," Luke said. He held out the box to Claire, and she picked a chocolate muffin.

There was another knock on the door, and Renee groaned, pulling off an enormous chunk of muffin and shoving it in her mouth. "Got it," she mumbled between crumbs.

Caleb swooped her up in a hug when she answered the door. He towered over her and had the muscles to toss her around like a doll.

"Hey," she squeaked.

"I can't believe you're here! And it's not Christmas Eve!"

"I know. Now, put me down."

Caleb let her go and stepped around her, taking a few strides across the living room. In the kitchen, he said hello to Claire and Luke. It was obvious they'd met before, as he teased Luke about volunteering for the holiday festivals.

"And I thought Claire was going to be there to keep me in line, but she had to zip down that bunny hill too fast and end up with a broken leg," Luke said.

Renee sat back in her chair and used the fork to cut off another chunk of the muffin. "How did you break your leg on the bunny hill? I didn't get the complete story."

"A picnic table," Claire said. "Wrong place, wrong time."

"Ouch."

"Sorry you're stuck with Renee, man," Caleb said, shrugging out of his jacket. He placed his coat on the back of Renee's seat and grabbed a coffee cup out of the drainer.

Renee looked at Luke. *Does he feel stuck with me?*

Luke smiled and laughed it off. "Claire assured me I'm in excellent hands. So, you have the tree with you? We can haul it up soon?"

"Yep." Caleb grabbed a muffin and sat down. "Let me finish this and the coffee and then we'll grab it. I'm not sticking around to decorate. Sorry to disappoint, sis."

"That's okay. I got Ney..." she cut herself off. "Renee. Lucky for me, Santa sent me a helper for the holidays."

"Does that mean I can skip the gift?" Renee asked, thankful Claire had stopped herself from using the childish nickname.

"Oh, no. You're on my couch; I get a gift."

Everyone laughed, and Renee sighed.

What a difference a week makes.

This time last Sunday, she was going over her notes for the executive readout, telling herself that impulsively kissing her boss would soon be forgotten and not affect her job.

No, she wouldn't get the Sunday jitters today. There was too much joy, fresh muffins, popcorn to string, and good-natured kidding around in her sister's apartment to be worried or stressed.

"Hey, turn it up. That's my favorite Christmas song," she said, hearing Bing Crosby's distinctive voice.

"Mine too," Luke said, pouring a cup of coffee.

"Careful," Caleb said. "'The Little Drummer Boy'" usually makes Renee cry."

"Same," Luke said, giving Renee a wink.

This guy is good-looking, charming, and bakes cheese-cakes. Why couldn't I find someone like him in Chicago?

Chapter Seven

Luke rushed from the high school to the town hall, where the final prep meeting was taking place. He glanced at the time on his cell phone as he entered the building with its "Welcome to Minier! We're excited to have you!" sign. He was ten minutes late, but he couldn't help it.

Inside the meeting room, he scanned the nine people assembled. The usual eight-person committee, headed by Alexis Tooley-Owens, and Renee, his partner-in-jingles, as he liked to think about her. He imagined her costume had bells attached to it, too.

Alexis was talking about the snacks for this evening's event. Luke didn't catch all the details, but he remembered cake pops being mentioned previously. He had contemplated volunteering to make them; cake pops were a fun challenge. He'd made them before, for a birthday party for his cousin Megan's daughter, Ella.

He glanced at Renee. She wore a deep-burgundy blouse and black slacks. Her honey-blonde hair was curled in thick, soft waves around her face, almost hiding small gold hoop earrings. There was a leather padfolio open in front of her, and he could see that she had already taken half a page of notes. She looked like she was ready for a boardroom, not the holiday festivity planning committee.

He looked at the clock on the wall. Yes, he was only ten minutes late. How could she have so many notes?

"Questions?" Alexis asked, glancing about the room. Everyone seemed to hold their breath. Her voice seemed clipped. Was she stressed about the first night?

"Not about cake pops," Renee said. Every head turned towards her.

"Well, what then?" Alexis shot back.

Renee put her pen down and clasped her hands together. "I am curious whether there have been any discussions about community service. I know the funds raised go towards the Christmas tree fund and the animal shelter, but I was wondering if we could do more. For example, a food pantry, or even building a little library-type pantry that wouldn't have to be staffed, just available for people in need, when they need."

Alexis held up a hand. "That's a great idea, but I'm afraid it's too late for this year. Maybe you'll stick around and help with next year's planning committee."

Luke noticed Renee blushed and noted the dig in Alexis's words.

Alexis continued. "We'll start up again in April. It takes a lot of work to pull this off, so we start early. But we all know you like to just ride in at the last minute and get all the glory."

"Whoa, now, ladies!" Andy Hill, the former owner of the hardware store, leaned forward and raised his hand. Luke felt like he was at school. "Let's keep it civil."

"Right, Andy," Alexis jumped in. "Let's get back on track." She asked Mrs. White about the printed partridge cards for the evening's activity.

Luke had been standing in the corner, not wanting to interrupt the meeting, but now he moved in and took a seat next to Renee.

Mrs. White explained the three different stations planned for the cards: one where the little kids could color, one where people could use watercolors to paint them, and one to be a glue and glitter station that Luke hoped he wouldn't have to approach too closely.

Luke reached over, took the pen that Renee had laid down on the pad of paper, and wrote, "I love the idea of a food pantry! Let's talk more and figure out how to make it happen. Maybe a meeting with the mayor?"

Renee leaned back in the seat next to him, seemingly at ease. She reached into her leather bag on the floor and grabbed another pen. She quickly wrote. "Good suggestion" under his scribble.

"Right, Luke?" Alexis called from the other end of the table.

"I'm sorry. I missed that."

Renee stiffened again.

"I wanted to check that you and Renee are all set with costumes and responsibilities for tonight. Do you have questions?"

"Well," he began, "I can't speak for Renee, but I'm all set, and the only question I have is for Mrs. White. Are you sure we need glitter and glue?"

Everyone laughed, and Mrs. White blushed. He enjoyed teasing her.

Once the room quieted down, he turned to Renee. "Do you have questions? Is your costume good?"

"No, I'm fine. It's going to be an outstanding event!"

Luke breathed a sigh of relief. He didn't think Renee was happy by any means, but she was playing nice.

Alexis finished running through the agenda and adjourned the meeting. As everyone mingled, Luke asked Renee if she'd like a ride to the library for the Partridge in a Pear Tree card-making event.

"No, I'll drive myself."

"I loved your idea about the food pantry and want to explore that more. Not sure we'll be able to talk during card making. Maybe we can get coffee afterwards?"

"At Gary's?" She glanced toward the front of the room where Alexis and Andy were talking. Gary's was the only place to get coffee in town. He didn't serve dinner but allowed customers to sit at the counter and drink coffee or eat any snacks they bought in the stations.

"She doesn't work nights," he said.

Renee's eyes darted to his. "It wouldn't matter if she did. It doesn't bother me."

He just nodded. He didn't believe her, but he wouldn't push it now. With time, he expected she would trust him and open up to him. People usually did.

"Gotcha. But coffee? Let's brainstorm a proposal to take to the mayor. I was thinking it might be a great tie-in to the scavenger hunt on Saturday. Bring a food item, get a hint at the first thing to find. Something like that. Off the top of my head."

Renee nodded, but the corner of her mouth dropped. "There's not much time to get information out."

"Hey, hey." Saying those words reminded him of Claire calling her NeyNey. He smiled. "I know someone who's exceptional at getting flyers out. And I hear she has some free time during the day."

"True." She nodded. "If I don't get called for an interview this week, that would work."

Right. She was job-hunting, but not for anything local. Luke needed to remember that and not get caught up in the whole goodwill towards men thing or the romance of the Christmas season. *Renee is here to help her sister out. That's it. Besides, she is uptight and bossy.*

"Luke? Can I talk to you?" Alexis called as he turned to leave.

"Sure thing. What can I do for you?"

Out of the corner of his eye, he watched Renee put on her black coat and fluff her hair before strolling out. He knew he didn't need to, but he'd wanted to walk out with her.

"You'll be dressed and at the library by five-thirty, right?" Alexis asked. "I know it doesn't start until six, but it's best that you're there and the kids don't see the elves arrive."

"Not a problem. I'll be there by five-thirty."

"Would you remind Renee, too? She flew out of here before I could catch her."

Luke didn't think Renee "flew" out of the meeting, but again, these two seemed to have some issues to work through. Maybe he'd get the chance to bring them together and smooth things over. He was used to doing that with teenagers, so surely he could do the same for two women a decade older than any of his students. It would probably be even easier.

Outside, Luke shrugged his coat on and looked up at the sky. Dark gray clouds were rolling in. It was going to snow. He hoped that snow wouldn't keep everyone from showing up at his first event as an elf.

Chapter Eight

Renee cinched her belt a little tighter. This elf dress had been made for her sister and was a little too big and a little too long on her. She pulled her hair forward so it would lie in front, then she adjusted her green and red hat. One last look in the library bathroom mirror, and it would have to do. She took extra time with her hair and makeup. She knew there would be pictures, and as ridiculous as she felt wearing the costume, she wanted to make sure everything was perfect. There would be evidence, AKA photos, and the internet could be brutal.

Exiting the ladies' room, she scanned the large open area with three long tables, familiarizing herself with the space. The planning committee had done a nice job setting up the room. It was clear to see that each table was designated for different age groups and their crafts. At the far end of the room was a refreshment stand with large glass dispensers of water, non-alcoholic eggnog, and a punch that was the same color green as her elf costume.

"Hey, hey, Ms. Elf!" Luke called from his spot next to the refreshments. She smiled to see him in the green velvet costume. It looked like a three-piece suit done up in elfin green with gold and red trim. His hat was like Santa's, with a long tail and a large three-inch bell on the end.

She walked towards him, shaking her head. "You look...like an elf from another planet, not the North Pole. What's with the suit?"

He smiled with that wide, open grin of his. "They suggested tights, and I threatened to quit. Suddenly, Mrs. White remembered this gem in her attic. Spiffy, huh?"

"I'm not sure I'd use the word spiffy. But if it makes you feel good, you're spiffy to the nth degree." She suddenly imagined him in a three-piece suit, black with a black tie. Wow. Her head spun as she imagined walking into a black-tie affair on his arm. Some hoity-toity corporate event or the wedding of a dignitary. It'd be a dream. She'd love for John to be there. If it made him jealous, it would serve him right. It was clear to see that Luke was much better looking and a more open, honest human being.

Stop right there, NeyNey.

"So." She had to change her line of thinking. "We need better names than Elf One and Elf Two or Mr. and Mrs. Elf." *Yikes! That was a poor turn of phrase.*

"For certain! Got any ideas?" His eyes sparkled with glee. It was too much.

"Well, how about calling me Holly and you Jolly?" she teased. He'd never go for it; it was too silly.

"Sweet! That's perfect. Wonder if we could get some name tags. But something special, not run-of-the-mill plastic holders with handwritten names. I've got an idea! I'll be right back."

He scanned the room, jogging over when he saw Mrs. White.

Renee glanced at the clock on the wall. They still had ten minutes before the event started. She spied Andy Hill across the room and went to get his input on the food pantry idea. If Alexis was going to cut her down without a discussion, she'd make the rounds with the other committee members to get their thoughts, and hopefully, get them on board.

An hour later, Renee squatted next to a little fellow who was coloring a holiday card. He had filled out the partridge shape with at least twelve different colors. It looked like a rainbow on steroids. "Wow, that is a beautiful bird. I love all the colors," she said to encourage him.

He looked up at her shyly. "You do? Thanks."

"Yes! You're very creative! Do you always use lots of colors?"

"Why have just one color when you can have all of them?" he replied.

"I agree!" Renee nodded. "I'm Renee. What's your name?"

"Easton."

"It's an honor to meet you, Easton. Who did you come with today?" Renee had noticed he'd been sitting alone coloring for a long time. No one seemed to pay attention to him.

"Mom."

"Who's your mom, Easton?"

"There." He pointed, and she followed the direction of his little finger. He pointed directly at Mrs. White, who was talking to Alexis.

"Mrs. White?" she asked incredulously. Mrs. White had to be eighty years old.

"No. Next to her."

"Ohh." Renee drew the word out. "Alexis. Of course. Did you know I went to high school with your mom?"

"How would I know that? I'm just a kid!" Easton laughed and shook his head.

Hearing her son laugh, Alexis rushed over. "How's it going, honey? Hi, Renee. I see you met my son."

"I did!" Renee smiled up at Alexis from where she was still kneeling beside Easton. "He's pretty cool."

Alexis looked down at her son's drawing. "Oh, Easton. Why did you use all those colors? We can't send that to Grandma now."

Renee fought the urge to stand up and throw a punch across the table at Alexis. "Are you kidding me? This is the very best picture I've seen all night! Easton's grandmother would certainly be proud of this artwork."

Easton had dipped his head at his mom's words but looked up at Renee. "You think so?"

"I know so. Shoot, I'd pay good money for that picture. It's the best partridge in a pear tree that I've ever seen!"

"Stay out of it," Alexis said through gritted teeth.

"How much?" Easton said at the same time.

"I've got a special coin in my shoe. You know, for emergencies. In case Santa's sleigh breaks down or something." Renee winked at Easton as she reached down to her shoe to grab the one-dollar coin. She loved the new these new

American Innovation coins, which honored innovations and innovators from each state. The 2024 Illinois coin, representing Illinois' farming tradition, was her favorite.

"You don't have to do that," Alexis said.

"I could make Grandma a boring one, Mommy," Easton said.

Renee laughed softly. "That sounds like a great solution, Easton. You're creative and a problem solver, too."

He looked tentatively at his mom. "Is that okay, Mom?"

"Yes," Alexis sighed. "That's fine." But she shot Renee a look that seemed to say, "This isn't fine, and it's not over."

Renee gave Easton the shiny gold coin, pointed out the plow, the prairie grass, the soil, and the bold "Illinois" at the top, and thanked him again before walking towards the refreshment table. She grabbed a red cake pop with a black belt around the middle and placed the picture under her coat.

"What do you have there?" Luke asked, drawing up alongside her.

"A gorgeous picture. Want to see?" She lifted her coat so he could see the colored picture underneath.

"Sweet! How did you get that?"

"Kind of a long story that's not endearing me to Alexis."

"Yikes." His eyebrows knitted together. "You two seemed to have a long history of not being on good terms."

"Hmm," she murmured. "Ten years? Maybe twelve. You could say that. I try to let go of those old hurts, but whenever I get within ten miles of this town, it's like a switch flips on and I'm reliving one of the worst days of my life all over again. I can't shake it."

"Do you want to shake it?" he asked.

"Of course I do." The urge to stomp her foot was strong, but she refrained. "It's been ten years. I shouldn't be stressing about stuff that happened in high school. My life is so busy I don't have time to think about it normally, but when I'm back here…"

"Maybe that's why you stay so busy. So you don't think about it?"

"Did we just start a therapy session? Am I on the clock?"

Luke looked around; the crowd was dwindling. They should mingle. "Well, not on a therapy clock, but we are on the elfin clock, so maybe we should talk to people. Make sure everyone's okay."

"Yeah, you're right. You get Alexis. I'll make the rounds." She bit into the cake pop and felt a rush as the sugary coating filled her mouth. "Oh, yum. These are so good."

"Not as good as mine," Luke said before walking off.

"You make cake pops, too?" *Is there anything this guy doesn't do?*

Back in Claire's apartment, showered and dressed in her flannel pajamas adorned with gingerbread people, Renee sat on the couch next to her sister.

Claire turned off the television—she'd been watching a college basketball game—and asked Renee how the evening had been.

"Fine. Civil. No fights broke out. There were no glitter spills. And the cake pops were a rush of sugar goodness."

Claire laughed. "Was there a risk of a fight breaking out? Do tell."

Renee pulled her hair back, twisting it so it lay loosely over her right shoulder. "You know, whenever Alexis and I are in the same room, there is a risk of a catfight."

"Ah, yes." Claire nodded. "The infamous Renee and Alexis battle for supremacy. Can't you just let it go?"

"She can't. I can't. The Universe refuses to. But on a happier note, I met her son tonight, Easton. He's the cutest. Gosh, I wanted to gobble him up. He had spiky blond hair and glasses, like the little boy in the "Jerry Maguire" movie. So cute. And he may be an artist. I bought the Christmas card he was coloring from him."

"You did?"

"Yep. Alexis seemed to be embarrassed by it. It was a multicolored rainbow gem of a little partridge. You know some kids color outside the lines? Well, this kid colors outside all boundaries. He used four different colors inside just one of the bird's wings. I think he was sent down from Venus, actually. Who is his father again?"

"Cole Owens. He's a piece of work. Last I heard, he was in the county jail for stealing from his grandmother."

"Wow, that's so sad. For Easton, Alexis, and Cole."

Claire nodded and stretched out her leg. "It is. So, did you get along all right with Luke? How did he do? I was hoping for a picture of him in his elf costume. Got one?"

"I do, but his costume is not as funny as it could be. It's like a leprechaun's suit."

"Oh, no! I wanted to see him in tights!"

"Oh!" Renee stopped scrolling long enough to look her sister in the eye. "You don't have a little crush on Mr. Luke, do you? Do you like him?"

Claire was shaking her head before Renee finished. "Oh, no. We're just friends. But we're friends who like to tease each other mercilessly. You wouldn't believe some of the nicknames he's given me since I broke my leg. He's a Pest with a capital P."

"Are you sure? Let's be honest here. You're single. He's single. You like each other. Maybe things..."

"No, that won't happen. I don't know how to make it clearer than that. He and I are not compatible that way."

Claire seemed serious. If her sister wasn't interested, then maybe she could move in for a little holiday fun. Nothing more than that, though.

"All right." Renee showed Claire the picture of Luke in his costume. Claire asked her to forward it. After clicking send, Renee continued, "I believe you. What's his story? He's very handsome and a nice guy. Why is he single?"

"I think he doesn't have much time. He moved here to take care of his dad, and it's a lot. We hang out at work, but not a lot outside of work."

"He's your work husband, then."

Claire laughed. "Maybe. He's so friendly, I bet everyone would consider him their work husband. Why all the questions? Do you like him?"

"Well, he is mighty fine to look at. And he's funny and kind. I have to work with him for the next eleven fun-filled nights; might be fun to have a romantic diversion."

"A romantic diversion, huh." Claire rubbed her thigh, just above the cast. "How's your love life been? You haven't mentioned dating anyone in a long time, but is there someone?"

"No!" Renee cried. "All the men I meet are married or jerks. Some are even married jerks."

Her mind shifted to Jerky-Jerk John. He should have made it clear that he was married before she kissed him.

"Is that so? Well, I hope your luck in that area turns around. But promise me one thing. Luke is a really good friend of mine. Whatever you do, don't break his heart. He's been through a lot, and I don't want to see him get hurt. So, divert with him, but don't forget you're not sticking around. Don't lead him on."

Renee yawned, and Claire got up on her crutches and made her way to her bedroom. Once she'd gone, Renee grabbed bedding from the closet and made her bed on the couch. It would have been nice if her parents' house was still available so she could have had her own room, but she was enjoying staying with her sister. She needed the time to reconnect.

Chapter Nine

Luke pulled into Gary's gas station ten minutes early. He glanced around before getting out of his car to make sure no kids were approaching. He didn't want any kids to become disillusioned at seeing an elf get out of a normal car. Plus, if he could avoid anyone seeing him in this costume outside of the actual festivities, it would be better.

Tonight's activity would be less hectic than the card-making the night before. They were making turtle candies, the pecan, caramel, and chocolate clusters, in Gary's kitchen. Gary's place didn't serve dinner, so it was a great kitchen to use for the Twelve Holly Dates of Christmas. Chorale students from the high school dressed in their Madrigal costumes would sing carols as townsfolk came in to buy the turtle goodies.

He and Renee would be Santa's chief candy makers tonight. Gary's cook, Alice, and her crew would be there as well, melting the caramel and chocolate and doing the prep and post-work in the kitchen while he and Renee hammed it up for the cameras out front.

Oh, and Alexis would be there, managing the cash box for this event since the town's holiday committee had paid for the supplies. After they reimbursed the holiday committee's fund for the expenses, the profit would go towards the town beautification fund. This year's fund was earmarked for painting the town's water tower, which was about fifteen years overdue for an overhaul.

Inside, Alexis and Renee were talking in low voices in the back corner. He searched their faces closely to read their moods. It seemed they were just talking, not arguing. Good sign.

He waved to Gary, who sat behind the register. Gary gave him a teasing, "Looking good!" shout, and Luke returned the sentiment. Even if Gary was in his usual gray flannel shirt, everyone could use a compliment.

"Evening, ladies. Is everything all right?"

Alexis turned to him first, and she had tears in her eyes. Oh, this wasn't as peaceful as it had first appeared. "Yes, things are great. We're all set. Alice's crew has everything ready to go. I have a special 'Santa's workshop is open' sign to hang on the door. I'll be back."

She rushed off, and Luke looked at Renee. "She's crying?"

"It's all right. We had a talk."

"Okay. Just checking. Thought I might have to intervene for a moment. Hey, I almost forgot. I have something for us."

"For us?"

"Yes." He held up a small paper bag. "I talked to Mrs. White last night about name tags. She pulled through in a big way."

He pulled out two bell-shaped fabric name tags. The bell background was red, and Mrs. White had embroidered their elf names, Holly and Jolly, in bright gold thread.

"Oh, my gosh. They are so cute!" Renee reached for the one that said Jolly.

"That's mine. You're Holly. I'm Jolly."

"Oh, right."

She winked at him, and Luke's heart jumped, reminding him of the Grinch when his heart started to grow.

Wow. Renee was always so put together. Tonight, her blond hair was braided, the ends were wrapped in thick red ribbon that was wavy on the edges. He couldn't think of the name for it, but he knew there was one. He had a sudden flash of memory of his mom sewing a baby quilt for someone and using a similar ribbon on the edges.

Wishing he could remember who the quilt was for, he wondered if it was still floating around the family somewhere. Maybe someday...he would have to ask his Aunt Mary if she remembered it.

"You going to put yours on, Jolly?" Renee finished pinning her tag on and looked at him.

"Certainly." He shook his head to clear the picture of a future baby wrapped in a blanket made by his mom. "Questions about tonight? We're actually making turtles. Well, not all of them. Alice and team have already made and packaged hundreds. We're really just part of the entertainment."

He walked behind the counter and assessed the placement of their tools. He swapped two bowls around; it was better to do the caramel first, then the chocolate.

"I don't know enough to ask good questions." Renee lifted her upturned hands. "Just tell me what I'm supposed to do. They obviously thought Claire would be here tonight; most of the town knows I'm useless in the kitchen."

"How would the town know that?"

"Hello?" She leaned her head towards him. "Small town calling. They know *everything*. And what they don't know, someone tells them within thirty minutes."

"Ah, so that's why you prefer the big city. No one to keep an eye on you."

Alexis returned to the cash box and said, "People are coming in. Ready?"

"We'll save that conversation for another time." Renee said, glancing up.

Luke could tell she was nervous about making the candies. Maybe there was some truth to her comments about her lack of skills in the kitchen.

She seemed to worry a lot about embarrassment. Well, he'd ham it up and make sure eyes were on him if Renee looked like she was unsure of herself.

Luke set up the system: he would arrange the pecans on a sheet pan lined with parchment paper, then pour melted caramel over their centers and hand things off to Renee to pour on the melted chocolate. How could she mess that up?

Two hours later, he had his answer when she missed setting the pan back on the hot plate securely, and hot melted chocolate ran all over the counter.

She looked at him with wide eyes, reminding him of Santa's reindeer, Rudolph. He stepped onto the lower shelf of the counter and raised his arms overhead, flapping them as if about to take off into the air. "Merry Christmas, everyone! Holly the Elf and I need to fly back to the North Pole. Several elves called off their toy-making shifts today because they overindulged in cake pops and eggnog at the holiday party last night, so Holly and I need to fill in. But don't worry, we'll be back down here in Minier tomorrow night, when we'll watch all of those French hens, and I know there are more than three of them, race around the pool. Don't forget the race is at six-thirty. Get there by six, so you can purchase your French hen and be entered into the race! Thank you all, and to all a good night!"

For good measure, he shook the bell on the end of his cap and pulled Renee into the kitchen.

"Clean up needed on aisle one!" he called. "We need an industrial cleaner and a lot of towels out there. Renee and I can't reappear until the people are gone or we'll blow our cover."

Alice ordered one of the kitchen helpers out to clean up. Laughing, Renee pulled Luke out the back door.

"Wow," she smirked. "That was some first-class thinking on your feet back there. Well done."

"I'm a high school teacher and a guidance counselor. I've been a real estate agent. Those are jobs that require you to react and pivot all the time. My middle name should be pivot."

"Jolly Pivot Woods. Got a nice ring to it."

Luke leaned against the brick wall and rubbed his arms. It was cold out here without a coat. "I'll file the paperwork to change my name next week. Wait, the week after. We have elf duty all next week."

Renee rolled her eyes and stomped her feet. "Let's go back in. Hopefully, everyone has left, and I can clean up my mess."

"Alice's crew may have it done already."

"I hope not. My mess. I should clean it."

Luke opened the back door and gestured for her to go in. As she passed, she laid a hand on his left bicep. He felt himself flexing. Ugh. What a muscle head move.

"Thanks again, Luke. I was mortified when the pan slipped."

"Not a problem. I've got your back."

She smiled, and he wanted to lean over and kiss her. *Whoa! Not appropriate to kiss an elf without permission.* He might get glittered or something.

Pulling into his father's driveway, he didn't see a light on inside the house. Luke sighed with relief. Dad must be asleep. Thank goodness.

Before he'd left for the night's holiday event, he'd made sure his dad had a hot dinner of stew and potatoes and a glass of milk. Dad had been contemplative tonight, thinking about Luke's early years, and he'd told Luke a story about his mom that he didn't remember.

Luke worried sometimes that his dad was trying to pass on all his memories before he died. Like he didn't believe he had months and years to impart those memories. Sometimes Luke found brief notes in his dad's house with a few keywords that his dad would expand into a story later.

The door to the garage, where Luke had his 'apartment,' was temperamental, and he had to give it a good push to get in. *Odd, the cold should have contracted the wood, not expanded it.*

Entering the single room that housed his kitchenette, bedroom, and living area, the day's tension eased. This had been home for eleven months now, and he was beginning to enjoy it. He missed the larger kitchen he'd had at his house in Springfield, but he'd sold the home when his dad got sick. He didn't mind. It was nice being close to his dad. The cancer was a bear, but it was good to share memories and even make some new ones with his dad while he could.

Once his dad fully recovered, he'd look for his own place. Much as he would have said 'never' just a few months ago, he was ready to settle down here. He was enjoying his teaching job and thought that maybe someday the real estate market would handle another agent. The newspaper reported that a new factory was being built in Bloomington, bringing well-paying jobs to the region. Maybe Minier would see a housing spike when the factory began hiring.

A neighbor had told him that the blue Victorian house with the white shutters on the corner of Minier Road and Maple Street was going on the market soon. It was a beautiful home—large, old-fashioned, with mature trees. Room for three or four kids and a couple of dogs.

Thinking about marriage and kids brought Renee to mind. He was thankful he'd stopped himself from kissing her or even reaching out and touching her face, which he desperately wanted to do tonight when she paused in the light under the back door. If only there'd been mistletoe, he would have had an excuse. He thought about the rest of the events on the calendar. He didn't remember mistletoe being mentioned for any of them, but maybe he should check with the committee. Mrs. White, or Andy, not Alexis.

He shook his head as he kicked off his elf shoes. *Stop that, Luke Woods. She is not interested in marriage. She's not even interested in living here. What are you thinking? As soon as the holidays are over, she's out of here, job or no job. She has an apartment waiting for her in Chicago. She's not staying here.*

Chapter Ten

Mayor Malloy sat behind his mahogany desk with a smile on his face, his wire-rimmed glasses propped high on his forehead. "Renee, you are a piece of work."

Luke chuckled from his seat as Renee took the state of Illinois map down from the wall across from the mayor's desk.

"I wasn't sure if you had projection capabilities. I'm glad I brought my own tools." Technically, the projector had come from her sister, who'd brought it home from the high school after Renee had pleaded for twenty minutes. The laptop was hers. "We'll be ready to go in just a few more minutes."

"As we wait for the power-point presentation, do you have any feedback for us on the holiday festivities so far?" Luke asked the mayor.

"It's been top-notch. The committee has done an excellent job. I'm hearing nothing but rave reviews."

"We've only completed two events so far. Let's not jinx it," Renee said as she sat back down and clicked the power button on the projector. "Perfect."

She swung in her seat and faced the mayor. "Here is an idea that the committee did not jump at. I think they're feeling the pressure and couldn't face a last-minute change request. So, I thought we would bring it to you, and if you approve, Luke and I will run with it from here, outside the committee."

"Well, I'm all ears," the mayor said, leaning forward. "This should be interesting."

"We propose a town pantry. Not a large affair. Not one that would require a manned operation or even a dedicated business space."

She clicked past her title slide and showed a list of county demographics, including median income, unemployment rates, and percentage in poverty.

"Here you can see that there is a need." Renee used a presentation clicker and advanced the slide. "Times have been hard since the meat-processing plant went out of business. A positive thing on many fronts, in my opinion, but not on employment."

The mayor nodded, and she clicked ahead. "As you can see here on this map, the nearest food pantry is in Bloomington, twenty miles away. That's not good enough," she continued. "We need to help our fellow residents, and we can."

She glanced at Luke. He raised an eyebrow at her use of the word "our". She would address that with him later.

She continued. "We propose an independent food pantry, which would be run like a Little Free Library. I was very excited to see we have three of those in town. This would be a Little Free Pantry, stocked with food."

"Hmm, interesting," the mayor said. "But it would need oversight."

"Yes, of course." Renee nodded. "Similar to how a Little Free Library has a caretaker, this would need one as well. My sister has volunteered to care for this pantry."

Again, Luke raised an eyebrow and tilted his head. *Well, she will when I ask her.*

"And what would the caretaker do exactly?" the mayor asked.

"Monitor the stock." Renee quickly advanced the slides to show one labeled "Caretaker Responsibilities". "Make sure no rotten or expired food has been put in it. Put out a call on the town's social media if supplies are low and need to be restocked. Ask for improvements. Identify whether the pantry needs any repairs."

"All right." Mayor Malloy nodded. "Good."

"Now, the thing we really need from you, Mayor, is permission to build at the location. I've been scouting out the village, and I think the perfect space is right outside of this building. On the west side, there is a space approximately two feet deep and six feet long that would be perfect for the pantry."

"And what would this pantry look like? How tall would it be?"

"Here is a drawing I made. I think it will work." Renee clicked through a few slides to show the model she'd made. "I need to talk to my brother to confirm it's doable. He's the carpenter, but I think it is."

"And your design," Mayor Malloy said, "looks like a...I can't think of the word."

"A Hoosier cabinet. Of course, we could come up with a few options and either take them to the town board for approval or somehow put it to a vote with all the citizens. But I was hoping for speed in all of this, so I proposed a design."

"Speed, huh?" Luke said, leaning forward.

She shifted in her seat. "Yes. It's Christmas. Wouldn't it be great if it were up and running by Christmas?"

"That's only..." The mayor glanced at the large calendar on the wall. "Eleven days away. Impossible."

"Not impossible." Renee shifted forward in her chair. "We would make a push during the Twelve Holly Days of Christmas festival to get donations. As a matter of fact, we have an idea to make it part of the Scavenger Hunt that happens on Saturday." It was Luke's idea—a brilliant one.

The mayor glanced at a large poster on his wall. It was a calendar view of the activities with notes on where he needed to be and when. "The Five Golden Rings event," he noted.

"Yes. We thought that the first thing on the scavenger list could be finding a canned or boxed good and having people bring that with them when they finish the hunt. Then we would have many items for the initial stocking of the pantry."

Luke chuckled. "A pantry stocking. For Christmas."

Renee glanced at him. *Now's not the time for cute jokes.*

The mayor wrote something on a sticky note and stuck it to the phone on his desk. "Has Alexis approved changing the scavenger hunt?"

"Not yet," Renee replied. "We'll see her tonight and discuss it."

"Where would we store everything until the pantry is built?"

Renee appreciated his serious questions and was thankful that she'd tried putting herself in the mayor's shoes as she prepared the presentation, anticipating his questions. She could answer this one.

"I talked to Bill in maintenance, and he said there's a storage room behind the public works building that could be used."

"Okay, good." The mayor nodded and his glasses slid forward. "I think this sounds great. I should run it past the town council first. Lucky for the two of you, we meet tomorrow morning. I'll call you after that meeting and confirm we're a go."

"Great. I'll leave my business card here." Renee reached into the outer pocket of her bag and set the card on his desk. "It has my number on it."

"Thank you both for the passion and conviction behind the idea. I don't know, Renee." He gave her a squint-eyed look. "I think you could be my successor. I've tried to get Alexis interested in the role, but she's adamant that it's not for her. Maybe it's for you."

She sighed. Her days of competing with Alexis were over. During their long chat at Gary's before the candy-making event, Renee had apologized for her part in their ongoing animosity, and Alexis had done the same. They were finally on their way to being friends again. "I'm flattered that you would say that, Mayor, but I'm not planning to move home."

"Very well."

They stood when the mayor did and said their good-byes. Outside, Luke gave Renee a high five. "Well done. I didn't think the slide deck was necessary, but you were right in putting it together. You convinced him. Now you have to convince Alexis."

"I'll talk to her tonight."

On the way to the evening's festival event, Renee called her brother Caleb and asked him about building the "Not-So-Little Free Pantry" for the town. He asked for general dimensions, location, and design ideas. He said it would be simple to build and that he could have it done in a week.

The rubber duck race, also known as the French Hen race, though the two birds looked nothing alike, was to be held at the community pool. It was just easier to buy three hundred rubber ducks versus searching for rubber French hens!

Luke and Renee changed into their elf costumes in their respective locker rooms. When Renee entered the warm and steamy pool area, she wished she weren't in a heavy, long-sleeved shirt, velvet vest, and thick tights. It was like walking into a sauna in long underwear.

Alexis was the point person for tonight's event. She was at the main table where people could buy a rubber duck for the race. Each duck/hen cost ten dollars, and the winner would win a gift basket filled with products and gift cards donated by various businesses in town.

All proceeds were going to Noah's Ark Animal Rescue, a non-profit, no-kill shelter.

It was a popular event. The prize basket was worth over six hundred dollars, and the two runner-up prizes were for gift cards to the grocery store in Mackinaw, a town ten minutes away. Everyone could use these prizes during the holidays.

Luke was talking to the men who would release the net holding the ducks at the starting line, and Renee made her way over.

"Hi, Holly!" Luke called as she approached.

"Jolly," she said with a nod. "Do you have a few minutes to talk to Alexis about the pantry?"

"Afraid to do so on your own?" he teased.

"You're a good buffer."

They approached Alexis, who was smiling ear to ear. There was a great turnout, and they were close to selling all 300 tickets. The race would begin in twenty minutes. Christmas music played, and the high school music director was prepping for a crowd sing-along.

"Alexis, could we talk to you for a few moments?" Renee asked as Alexis wrapped up a conversation.

"Of course...Holly," she said, reading the name tag.

Renee gave her a half-smile. "We met with the mayor today about the pantry, and he loved the idea."

Alexis' brows dipped in the middle in apparent irritation. "You went behind my back, Renee?"

"No. I came to you first. You didn't want to consider it, so I went to the mayor. He still needs to get it approved by the council, but if they approve, we're going to tweak the scavenger hunt and ask people to find and bring a food item. That's it. That's the only change to the festival that affects the festival committee. We'll take care of collecting and storing the food, and I'm working on the build-out with my brother."

"Oh." Alexis paused, considering. "Well, if that's all, that's not so bad. We can manage that. It's a good idea, Renee. There are many people who could use the help."

Is she serious? No fight? Must be because Luke is here. "Great. I'm glad you're good with it. Hey, how's my buddy, Easton? Is he here tonight?"

Alexis smiled. "Front row." She pointed towards the stand. Easton was sitting with Alexis's sister, Lorraine.

"Cool." Renee checked the clock on the wall. They still had ten minutes. "Will it be all right if we go talk to him?"

"You're his current hero for buying his art." Alexis' tentative smile didn't reach her eyes. "It's fine."

Luke touched Renee's arm. "I'm going to pump up the crowd."

"Thanks, Alexis. Ok, Jolly." Renee strolled towards the young boy and his aunt, scanning the crowd as she passed. "Hey, Easton! Hi, Lorraine."

"Hi," Easton said in a soft voice, looking up at Renee with his big blue eyes and pink cheeks.

Renee kneeled in front of him. "Are you ready to yell really loud to help the hens race?"

Easton looked past her to where all the ducks were bobbing in the water, just under the swimmers' starting blocks. When it was time for the race, the net would drop into the water and a large oscillating fan would push the floating duckies to the finish line, which was three feet shy of the other end of the pool.

Easton nodded and looked back at Renee. "Yep." He held up a piece of paper. "We're number one-oh-nine," he declared, pronouncing each number separately.

"Well, good luck, Number 109! I'm so glad I got to see you today. I have to get back to work. Have fun." Renee looked at Lorraine. "Your nephew is so cool."

Lorraine laughed. "I know. Nice to see you, Renee. Better you than me in that outfit." She patted her belly, which was undoubtedly incubating a tiny human.

Renee laughed. "I'd love to see it. Congrats."

She stood and glanced towards the ticket table where Luke was greeting people as they entered and purchased their duck tickets. She approached the music director, who'd just stood to lead the choir.

"Hi, Mr. Feno," she said.

"Why, hello." He paused, glancing at her name tag. "Holly!" He gave her a wink.

His bushy white eyebrows reminded her of Santa Claus, and she bit her tongue not to call him that in front of the crowd.

"Want to help lead the chorus in singing Rudolph?" he asked.

"No one wants to hear me sing!" Renee smiled. Movement to her right caused her head to turn. Luke was flapping his arms, trying to get the crowd to start a wave as if they were at a baseball game.

Renee nodded at him, and standing next to Mr. Feno, she started the arm gesture to get this part of the crowd going. Soon, the entire crowd was singing about reindeer and whooshing up out of their seats to do the wave.

Once the song ended, Renee glanced at Luke. He was moving towards her; his smile lit up the room brighter than Rudolph's nose on the darkest Christmas Eve.

"Looks like it's time," Luke said, touching Renee's lower back.

"Let's do it!"

Alexis asked Renee and Luke to pace in front of the crowd; she would go to the finish line and announce the winning numbers. If needed, a net on a long pole would remove the ducks from the pool.

Speaking into a cordless microphone, Alexis asked the crowd, "Are you ready?"

Excited shouts filled the room.

"All right!" Alexis called. "Let's count it down!"

She began counting backwards from ten, and the crowd screamed the numbers with her.

Luke and Renee gestured wildly, fanning the crowd's eagerness for the race.

As soon as Alexis yelled, "Go!", the two men dropped the net, and one of them turned on the six-foot tall fan. It took a couple of seconds, but the rubber ducks started slowly moving forward.

Renee was closer to the finish line than Luke, and she watched him circle his arm widely, encouraging the little inanimate ducks to hurry along. Renee approached Alexis near the finish line.

"Nice job getting the crowd fired up," Renee said to her former frenemy.

"Wasn't too hard. They're anxious." Alexis smiled at her.

They watched as the ducks crept closer and closer to the finish line. All eyes were on the ducks in the lead, floating across the pool, bopping like they were in no particular rush to get anywhere.

The crowd kept cheering, "Go!" and "Come on!" and "Hurry it up!"

Renee looked for her co-elf and found Luke mock-running alongside the pool. She laughed and shook her head. As ridiculous as she felt in the costume, she pushed aside the embarrassment and embraced the moment. She was here, making memories. The joy of Christmas, a community coming together in the holiday spirit, smiling and hugging their neighbors; what was not to like about this?

Two rubber ducks inched towards the finish line, and Renee cheered along with the room full of townspeople.

A few moments later, the ducks crossed the finish line, half an inch separating them. Renee leaned closer to see the winning number, but the ducks were about seven feet away. She turned her head to look for the net when "whack!" something hit the back of her legs, and she whirled her arms to keep her balance.

"No, this isn't happening!" she yelled, fighting to regain control of her balance.

"Holly!" Luke was yelling at her, and she turned her head towards him as her arms continued their frantic flapping.

It was inevitable; there was no way she could right herself, and she splashed into the pool. The crowd let out a collective gasp just before she hit the water.

Sputtering, she surfaced and kicked her legs to get to the edge. One elf slipper slipped off her foot. She swam to the edge and grabbed on, spitting water.

Luke reached down to grab her hand; she shook her head no.

"I'll climb up the ladder," she said. She held on to the edge and moved towards the ladder. The water weighed down the velvet and cotton outfit; each movement took extra effort.

Someone ran out of the boys' locker room with a stack of towels.

"Are you alright?" Alexis asked, leaning towards Renee.

Renee squinted at Alexis and contemplated whether she could pull the other woman into the water with her if she asked her for a hand climbing out.

She glanced at the crowd. *With three hundred witnesses? That wasn't a good idea.*

"I will be," she muttered, climbing up. "What happened?"

"I'm sorry," Alexis whined as Luke handed Renee a large towel. "I was trying to pull out the winning duck, and I didn't realize how close you were."

Wrapping herself in the towel, Renee looked at Alexis. Worry furrowed her eyebrows, and the corners of her eyes turned down. She looked honestly remorseful.

Luke stepped closer, listening to the conversation. "Why don't you go dry off and change? We can wrap this up."

Renee looked at the crowd. There were smiles everywhere she looked. If she stormed out of here, they would assume she was embarrassed, and she'd never hear the end of this. On a positive note, maybe this debacle would finally put an end to the humiliation of getting dumped at prom.

She sighed. Best to play it off as no big deal. She smiled at Easton, who was standing with a worried look on his face. She slipped her arm out of the towel and gave him a wave and a thumbs up. "I'm okay!" she shouted, and the crowd roared.

Luke leaned towards Alexis. "You didn't announce the winning numbers."

"Oh, right!" She pulled the net to her and reached for the duck. "Why don't you announce it, Holly?"

Alexis turned the microphone on and held it up to Renee. Renee read off the number. "Two eighty-eight!"

A loud cheer rang out along with a room full of groans.

Renee seemed to be energized by the noise; the corners of her mouth curved upward. When she went into the water, he assumed she'd come up and demand someone get fired. She seemed like the type. Type "A" for aggressive. But her refusal to rush into the locker room surprised him. She stood straight, head back, though no longer sporting the jazzy elf hat. He looked in the pool; her hat and shoe floated in the water. He hoped she didn't have her cell phone tucked into a pocket.

"What about second and third?" someone yelled.

The three looked at the pool. The second duck was easy to see; it was the only other duck past the finish line indicator. Alexis handed the pole to Luke, and he fished the duck out and handed it to Renee.

"Ninety-seven!"

Another cheer.

Everyone watched as the third-place duck inched towards the finish line.

"Go, little duckie, go!" Luke shouted.

"Go! Go! Go!" Renee chanted. She turned to the audience and raised her fist, continuing the chant. The audience joined her.

The puddle around her feet inched towards his shoe. He caught her eye and smiled. Water from her drenched hair continued to stream down her face and the side of her neck.

She had to be miserable, but she smiled for the crowd and looked like she was having the time of her life.

The third duck finally crossed the finish line, and the crowd let out an enthusiastic roar. It was further away than the first two, and Luke leaned forward to inch the net closer to it.

"Careful, Jolly," Renee said, gripping his arm. "You don't want to end up soaked like me."

The image of the two of them diving into the pool together flashed through his mind.

"It could be a new elfin sport," he said, smiling.

Renee giggled. "We'd need new material for our costumes. Something that won't shrink when wet."

Luke shook his head to get the image of Renee's shrinking dress out of his mind. "Got you," he said, getting the net under the duck.

He pulled it in and let Renee pluck it out of the net. She turned towards Alexis, who still held the microphone. "Number one fifty-nine."

A woman in a knitted vest with a strand of electric Christmas lights that were flashing in a steady on-off-on-off pattern stood and waved her ticket.

Alexis waved to the woman. "Thank you, everyone! Will the three winners meet me at the ticket counter for their prizes? And a reminder for everyone: tomorrow night is Four Calling Birds, where the kiddos can come to the library to write their letters to Santa! We'll have hot chocolate and snacks. Holly and Jolly will be there with several members of the festivity committee. Don't miss it!"

She turned off the microphone and looked at Renee. "Go change, Renee. We can handle it from here."

"Gladly." Her eyes widened, and she shivered. "See you guys tomorrow night."

She turned and walked to the ladies' locker room.

Tomorrow night could not come soon enough for Luke. The more time he spent with Renee, the more he wanted. Her spirit and tenacity constantly surprised him. She was a rare gem, and he looked forward to discovering all he could about her.

Chapter Eleven

Renee scanned the library meeting room. Large snow globes with constant movement lined the conference tables, a pretty, decorative touch. Stacks of decorative paper lay at the ends of each table where the kids could grab them on the way to their seats. Once they wrote a letter to Santa, they would put it in a pre-addressed envelope marked simply "North Pole," and drop it into a large mailbox brought in specifically for this event. Not an official U.S. Postal Service mailbox, but a repurposed out-of-commission mailbox that someone had painted red and decorated with images of holly and a snowy scene with a post office building marked "North Pole."

Luke had reminded her that when the kids dropped their letters in the mailbox, they would receive a Santa Claus ornament to take home. They would have to monitor the mailbox as they walked around, helping the kids with their letters.

Everything appeared to be in order. Committee members readied the room; Renee just had to show up in costume and be jolly. No, Holly.

Luckily, her costume had survived the dunk in the pool, washing, and drying with no apparent shrinkage.

It was a good thing, because she did not have time today to run to town to find a new costume. She'd scoured job boards, sent emails to acquaintances, and personalized forty-seven query letters.

Before starting on actual job applications, she'd created a spreadsheet to track all the job-search activities. It'd been a few years since she'd been on the hunt for a job.

She was pleased with her progress. Only nine days after leaving her former employer, she'd submitted almost one hundred applications. Now, if only a few of those would start turning into interviews.

"Hey, Holly!"

Luke's voice preceded her setting eyes on him. She turned around in a circle, searching for him.

"Luke?" she called when she didn't see him. "Where are you?"

"Oh!" His head popped up from under a table. "Here! I saw your shoes, so I knew it was you."

His dark brows raised in a friendly greeting, and his elf hat sat a little lopsided on his head.

"Were you taking a nap?" she asked as she stepped around the conference table to approach him.

He winked while rising to his feet. "Not a good one. Just trying to center myself before the craziness begins."

Renee reached up to straighten his hat. Mission accomplished, she gently smoothed strands of his hair, pleasantly surprised by the softness. She had a feeling he was a few weeks past a trim, but she liked the shaggy look on him.

His eyes seemed to examine her face, searching for something. She dropped her hand and turned towards the table, straightening a group of crayons.

"Not a bad idea," she said, avoiding his eyes. "It's a good thing this is a quick event; I'm a little tired myself."

"Busy day watching TV?" His voice held a smile. He was teasing, not mocking.

"No!" Her head jerked towards him. "I was very busy applying for jobs. I'm not sitting around eating chips and watching Netflix."

"Hey." He held up his hands. "Just joking with you. How's the job search going?"

"Slow. I attribute that to the season. People are thinking about the holidays and taking time off. I expect it will pick up in January. I'm just thankful I had a place to land."

"At your sister's?"

"Yes. Well, I mean, she needed me. Otherwise, I could have stayed home to job hunt."

"Where's home?" he asked.

"Chicago."

"I knew that, but where do you live in the city?"

"Oh, sorry. Bucktown."

"Nice."

"Expensive."

"Is that a brag?"

"No, just reality." She sighed. "Unfortunately, if I don't get a new, high-paying role soon, I'm going to have to think about moving somewhere further from downtown." She shivered.

"Rent's that bad?" he asked. "Or do you own your place?"

"Rent. I wish I'd had the foresight to buy a few years ago."

The conference room door opened, and Mrs. White entered. "Hello, our friendly elves!"

"Hi, Mrs. White," they replied in unison.

"There's a line forming outside. Are you ready for the kiddos?"

Renee looked at Luke. "Ready, Jolly?"

"For certain! Let's go!"

Every time Renee was with Luke, it was like she was peeling off the layers of a plastic-wrapped gift ball, like the one in the family game played at Christmas last year, where you had to peel off the plastic while wearing kitchen mitts. If you released a treasure before the next person in the circle rolled a seven on a pair of dice, it was yours. Otherwise, you passed the ball and the mitts to the next person.

Luke was a multi-layered mystery. She couldn't wait to find out more, but for the next two hours she had to be Holly the Elf.

Luke moved to the front of the room and began high fiving the kids as they entered. He then pointed to the seats and told them to find a seat and write their letter to Santa.

Renee moved around, pointing out the paper and pencils and crayons to the kids. If they didn't have a parent with them, she would ask them if they could write or needed help.

When Easton entered the room with Alexis, she followed him to his seat to encourage him. He said he was sad because he hadn't won the French Hen race, and Renee explained it was a game of chance, not certainty.

"Okay," he said, drawing out the word to last four whole seconds. "I understand."

"Good. Now, what are you going to ask Santa for in your letter?" Renee asked, kneeling next to him.

"Can it be a secret?" His pleading eyes nearly broke her.

"Oh, of course. What you want is between you and the big man. Good thing you can write. You don't have to share it with anyone. Maybe you can even draw a picture for Santa of what you want. You're so creative."

"That's a good idea, Miss Holly."

"I'll let you get started, Easton. See me when you're ready to mail your letter. We have a little gift for you to take home."

"With certainty?"

"With certainty."

Renee moved along the row of kids who were happily writing and drawing on their letters to Santa. She reached the end of the row, where Luke stood.

"Certainty, huh?" he said.

"You heard that?"

"Sure. We're all searching for certainty. It was a nice touch, Holly."

He turned and walked towards the mailbox, where a young girl with bright red hair in a long braid down her back stood, ready to mail her letter.

Renee was certain she needed a job. And she was certain she was thankful she had this volunteer activity to help fill her time. Renee wondered why Luke had entered her life at this moment.

Sometimes she liked to believe the universe was working magically, especially at Christmastime.

Was there a grander purpose in her ending up here, now? She still flushed with embarrassment thinking about kissing her boss and finding out he was married. If you'd asked her last month if she would ever quit her job, she would have laughed in your face.

But here she was. No job. Sleeping on her sister's couch. Playing the role of "Holly the Elf".

The universe was full of surprises and sometimes magic. Maybe Jolly the Elf, AKA Luke, had a role to play in her life that was bigger than co-host of the Twelve Holly Days of Christmas celebration in Minier.

It sounded like a change in trajectory had brought him here recently, too. His dad must be really sick if Luke had changed careers to take care of him.

Renee hoped she'd learn more about Luke's situation at some point, but when they were together at these events, they were busy interacting with community members, ensuring all were having a great time.

Maybe it was time for Renee and Luke to have some fun that didn't involve green costumes and bells that jingled.

As Luke pulled into their shared driveway, he noticed the living-room light glowing in his dad's house. Typically, his dad was upstairs in bed by 9:00 PM. He said that with his medication, he couldn't keep his eyes open long enough to watch the ten o'clock news anymore.

I hope he's all right. Better check.

Luke got out of the car and took a deep breath. The air was cool, not cold yet, and it energized him. Thankfully, it was Friday night, and he could sleep in on Saturday if needed. If his dad was having a rough night and needed looking after until late in the evening, Luke could handle it.

Walking up the steps to the back door, Luke rolled his ankle on a broken piece of concrete. He shook his head, mad at himself for not paying more attention. He knew the rough spot was there. Hoping he'd just tweaked his ankle and had no serious damage, he opened the screen door and tried the door handle of the main door. Unlocked. Not good.

Entering the back foyer, he flipped on the exterior light. He'd need the illumination when he left.

He strolled through the kitchen, which could use a fresh coat of paint and new curtains. With his dad's cancer battle, he knew it wasn't something to be concerned about right now, but he hoped to spruce it up in the spring.

"Dad?" he said quietly, entering the living room.

The TV was on, but no sound came from the set. His dad was lying on the couch, a blanket covering him, eyes closed.

The sound of Luke's voice roused him, and he sat up slowly. "Luke? What time is it? Is it morning?"

Luke pulled off his coat and sat in the worn, tweed recliner. He'd tried to buy his dad a new one, but his dad wouldn't hear of it. "No, Pops, it's nine-thirty at night. You fell asleep on the couch."

Michael leaned over and turned on a lamp, illuminating the room with a soft glow. He looked at Luke and scoffed.

"Why, it's Santa's little helper. Don't you look adorable."

Luke chuckled. "Thanks. That's what I was going for. Adorable. Like a kitten."

"Precious. How were tonight's festivities?" Before he finished the question, his body shook with a drawn-out cough.

Luke waited for the cough to subside before answering. It was painful to listen to the deep cough that shook his dad's whole body.

"It was good. Kiddos wrote letters to the dude at the North Pole. Pretty easy gig. Not as eventful as last night's."

He thought about Renee falling into the pool and climbing out soaking wet, her exaggerated makeup smeared around her eyes. She was still confident, gorgeous, and feisty.

"Yeah? Good."

"Why are you sleeping on the couch? You all right?"

Michael leaned back and shut his eyes. "I didn't have the energy to get myself up to bed. I was going through old papers, shredding them, and guess I overdid it."

"Why didn't you wait until I could help with that?"

"I can't have you waiting on me. I have to get back to doing stuff around the house. If I'm not useful to myself or anyone else, might as well put me out to pasture."

Luke chuckled. His dad was a retired insurance sales agent, but he liked to use farming references, which cracked Luke up.

"That's true." His dad preferred it when they could joke about dying; if the mood got too heavy, he'd either make a joke or shut down. "On a positive note, it's good you were up to the task of starting it."

"Yeah." Michael nodded. "I felt pretty good today. Even walked around the yard for a few minutes, looking at everything that needed to be done before winter sets in. I made you a list."

Luke laughed outright. "Good. I'll get on it this weekend. Glad to hear you got outside."

Michael was self-conscious about his slow pace and inability to stride about outside. He worried the neighbors would take pity on him if they saw him walk four steps and rest, catching his breath. Luke understood where his dad was coming from, but he worried that if his dad didn't get out and get fresh air, it would do more harm than feeling slighted over how the neighbors might perceive him.

"Yeah. Well." He tossed off the blanket. "Think you can give me a hand walking up the stairs?"

"Sure, Pops. Glad to."

The narrow staircase was difficult to navigate side by side, so Luke had to walk up sideways with his dad's arm over his shoulder, but they made it to the top, and Michael shuffled into his bedroom.

"Hey," he said, tossing his glasses onto the nightstand. "I've been meaning to ask. How are things working with Claire's sister? What's her name?"

"Renee." *Though I call her Holly more than Renee.* "Things are good. She's always on time, gives one hundred percent, and she's friendly. She's a good partner."

Michael nodded his head. "A good partner, you say? Good to hear. Maybe one of these days you'll find a proper partner. You deserve love and all that goes with it, son."

He looked at the picture of his wife, Lisa, on the night-stand. "Your mom and I would love to see you married before you're forty."

"Ha. I'm too busy taking care of you, old man. Let's get you back to full health, and then we can discuss my love life."

"We only get one life, kid, don't put off the important things."

"You're important to me. Now get some sleep."

Luke turned and walked down the stairs. *It's strange taking care of the ones that raised you,* he thought, as he sensed the progression of the school-pictures years moving backwards in time as he descended the stairs. *We start out being cared for, then we grow up and do the caring.*

Entering his apartment behind the garage, he pulled off the elf costume and hung it up, spraying it with fabric freshener. After Saturday's event, he planned to wash it thoroughly.

As he stepped into the shower, his dad's comment about finding a proper partner came to the forefront of his mind. It had been a few years since he'd had a serious girlfriend. He'd been too busy building his realty business in Springfield.

Maybe his dad was right. He was putting his life on hold until...until what? Until everyone was healthy? Until he had enough money in the bank? Until he'd accomplished a few more career goals?

Renee seemed to be the type of person to have a life map with each milestone properly defined by objective success criteria. Something he might have encouraged the high schoolers he counseled to do but had never done himself.

Was now the time to put some goals on paper?

Like opening his own bakery?

That goal seemed too far-fetched. He hadn't even confessed his love of baking to anyone yet. His dad thought he did it to remember Luke's mom. That had started his love of baking, but it was fully his own now.

After the shower, he crawled into bed with a blank notebook and a pen. It was time to write out some new goals. Asking Renee on a date was the first thing he listed.

Chapter Twelve

Renee arrived at Town Hall thirty minutes before the scavenger hunt was to begin so she could put out empty boxes to accept the canned and dry goods that people would gather during the hunt.

She and Claire had created signs for the boxes to show everyone where to place the donations. Moving a large conference table outside onto the sidewalk in her elf shoes was not the easiest task of the day, but she got it done.

Luke approached as she was pulling the table legs out. "Need a hand?" he asked.

"Please!"

They set up the table, and she placed the box of scavenger hunt sheets on top of it. "We need to get chairs. Someone will need to sit out here for the duration."

"We assigned people to time slots, right?" Luke asked, following her inside the building.

"Yes, the list is in that box. I don't think Alexis will be here today. She said she has a family something she couldn't miss."

"Too bad. You won't get to see Easton."

Renee turned to Luke and smiled. "It's pretty obvious, huh?"

"Yeah. He's charmed you good."

The door was heavy, and she grunted when she pushed it open. "Hey," Luke said. "How did you get that table outside by yourself?"

"Determination."

You just have to set your mind to it, and ninety-five percent of the time, you could pull it off. That had been her motto since grade school. She might not be the smartest, fastest, or prettiest, but she could study, endure, or put on makeup.

"You've got a boatload of determination," Luke said, reaching for folding chairs. "Are three chairs enough?"

"Should be."

Renee grabbed the signs and boxes she'd brought with her and turned to go back out. She hadn't wanted to leave them outside unattended while she struggled to get the table set up.

"Think we'll have a lot of participants today?" Luke asked.

"No idea. Everything has been pretty packed so far, but it's one of the last Saturdays before Christmas, so people might be going shopping."

"Good point. Too bad there aren't more shops in town."

"Too small to support a lot of retail." Renee set two boxes on top of the table and affixed signs with paper tape.

Luke opened the chairs and placed them behind the table. "Sad to see so many empty shops on Main Street."

"Yeah. I know. I'm sure as a realtor that really piques your interest."

"Of course," he said. "I haven't found a seller willing to talk about them, either. I was thinking about maybe buying one and creating pop-up shops. Seasonal things. Like gifts and wrapping during the holidays, seasonal decorations."

"That sounds...random."

"You're right. Too random. Maybe the space could be rented out for parties, showers, special meetings."

"But there are rooms to rent at the library and the town hall."

"Yes, and they could use a little rehab."

"True. I swear I can still smell cigarette smoke in the town hall building. And it's been a non-smoking space for years." She stepped back to check out her work. The signs were legible, cute, and direct. Perfect.

Luke laughed. "Right."

"I think it's great that you're brainstorming options, though, for the empty storefronts." Renee looked at the sad, aging buildings around them. "It would be good to see the town reinvent itself. If you could draw some businesses to come here, you'd have to convince the residents that it's in their best interest to spend money here. So many people work in Bloomington or Peoria that they do their shopping while they're there and then they just go home when they get back to Minier. I get it, too. When you've driven thirty to forty minutes to get here, once you hit the town limits, you just want to be home."

Luke nodded, the ball at the end of his hat bouncing with the movement. "Maybe the pop-up idea would work on the weekends."

"It's a lot of rent to pay for space if you're only open two days a week. And if someone like you did that, you'd never have a day off! You'd work at the school Monday to Friday and then work in the shop on weekends. It's too much!"

His mouth twisted. "I bet you work a lot of hours. I mean, worked."

"Sure. But I would try to work it to where I had the weekends off. I'd rather work five twelve-hour days during the week and have the weekend off than have to work weekends. Weekends are mine." She pointed at herself with her thumb.

"That's great." Luke pulled a clipboard from the box of supplies. "Here's the volunteer schedule." He placed it on the table. "What are your weekends like? When you're working, not while you're here."

He smiled, and Renee wanted to enter a staring contest. His eyes were the kindest, most unassuming she'd ever seen. He must be a fantastic student counselor.

She blinked and reminded herself what his question had been. "Right. Weekends. Saturdays are for hanging out, going to shows, museums, and brunch with friends. On Sundays, I prep for the week ahead. Laundry, house stuff, pay bills. That way, I can focus on work during the week."

"So that sounds like a single day off. Not two, if you're working all day Sunday."

"Hmm. Never thought about it like that. It's just my routine." She shrugged and looked at the time on her phone. She glanced up and down the street. "People should arrive soon. I hope it's busy today, so we can fill up these boxes with food donations. My brother Caleb is working on the pantry, and I think he'll have it ready by Christmas."

"That's great, just when people can use it."

"Unfortunately, we won't have hams or turkeys in it, but if people are in need, they can get some staples.'

"For certain."

Three teenage girls walked up, all wearing ugly Christmas sweaters. "Hi, Mr. Woods," the first one said. Her sweater sported a plaid reindeer.

Luke threw up his hands, like the last thing he'd expected was to see people he knew today. "Rebecca, Trina, and Amanda. How are you? Ready for the hunt?"

"We are!"

Luke clapped. "I'll get you registered. Holly can explain the rules."

Renee stepped forward. "Have you done this before?"

The girl with the Mrs. Claus sweater nodded. "A dozen times."

"So you know the rules. We give out the instructions at three-fifteen, after everyone is checked in. The first team or person back is the winner. Please note on the list, when it says to find and bring back a canned or other non-perishable food item, it means really bring one back, not a picture of it. We're building a food pantry for residents."

"Cool. Are the five golden rings new this year?" the third teen asked. Her sweater made her look like a Christmas tree with working lights and ornaments.

Each year, the festival committee made and hid five gold rings around town besides other scavenger clues. Sometimes the "ring" was a car tire painted gold, or a bike wheel, or a hula hoop propped in a storefront window. Contestants had to decipher a clue, find the intended item—ring or other clue—and take a picture on their phone.

"They're new every year. I think they're going to be tough this year, but you can be the judge of that. Good luck. And remember to return by 5:00 PM, whether or not you've completed the list. We don't want teams wandering around after dark."

"Gotcha," the first girl with the plaid reindeer sweater said.

Luke signed them in as a team as other people approached. Soon, both Renee and Luke were checking in contestants and explaining the rules. Bringing back a physical item was confusing to some of them, but once they understood what it was for, they were all for it.

The mayor was present at three-fifteen to officially start the Five Golden Rings Scavenger Hunt. He yelled, "Go!" and there was a flurry of clue lists being handed out to each team or participant.

A few moments later, all the teams were off, and Renee stood with her hands on her hips, watching the last team depart.

"Wow. That was a lot," she said, shaking her head.

"It's like dropping food into a lake and watching the fish start a feeding frenzy."

"I guess so; can't say I've done that."

"I haven't either, but I've seen videos." Luke sat down and sighed. "Now we wait."

Renee reached down and opened a "toolbox" that she'd labeled "Elf's Tools", but which really housed her SLR camera. "I'm going to take a few pictures. We won't see a team return for at least thirty minutes."

"You're a photographer?" Luke asked, leaning forward in his chair.

Renee flicked the switch, popped the cover off the lens and twisted it. "Hobby." She shrugged.

"Nice camera."

"Smile," she said, aiming it at him.

He smiled, and she loved being able to hide behind the camera as she studied his face. Twisting the lens to blur the background, she took another picture. "Don't smile," she commanded.

Luke tried to look serious, but there was laughter in his eyes. She snapped another picture. "Can't you be serious?" she asked.

"Not when you have me feeling like a fool. Couldn't you take some pictures when I'm not in this elf getup? I look ridiculous."

"You're playing a part, Jolly. Go with it. What would an elf do?"

She kept snapping as he talked. She normally took photographs of buildings, landscapes, and interesting objects; people were too hard for her to capture. They moved too much, were too self-conscious and nervous. She could never get them to relax enough to make interesting art.

But she was going to enjoy studying these pictures later. She wished she could take pictures of Luke in his normal clothes, not the dark green suit, silly hat, and curly shoes. Those were fun, but he couldn't relax enough for her to get a great shot. And she wanted a great shot.

A picture of Luke would be fun to have when she was back in Chicago, grinding away at some soul-sucking corporate position so she could afford her rent and weekly manicures.

Luke stood. "All right, that's enough. Unless I get to take pictures of you in your silly costume, you need to find something else to shoot."

Renee laughed. "Gladly, I prefer to take pictures of things, not people. I'll be back in a few minutes."

Luke watched Renee walk north, towards the downtown storefronts. A beauty salon, a custom T-shirt shop, and a regional newspaper office were the only businesses on the two-block stretch.

Wow. Photography. Never would have guessed.

He'd love to see her work. Would it be dull or full of life? Artsy or serious? Did she share her photography? Would she do family portraits if asked?

He wanted some pictures taken with his dad. He couldn't remember the last time they had taken photos together. Probably college graduation. Over seven years ago.

Time to change that.

Renee might not do it, but it wouldn't hurt to ask.

Mayor Malloy exited the building and called a cheerful goodbye to Luke.

Luke tore his eyes away from Renee. "Have a nice evening, Mr. Malloy. Do you want me to text you when we lock up the building?"

"No need. I trust you." He paused and looked up the block at Renee, who'd stopped to take a photo of something on the sidewalk. They were too far away to see what it was. "And her," he said, walking towards his car. Before he got to the parking lot, he turned back to Luke. "You know, she's pretty special. Don't you think?"

"I...uh..."

The mayor laughed and turned away. "Precisely, Luke. Precisely."

Looking at Renee's retreating back, he thought about the way she'd outlined her proposal to the mayor, with a slide deck presentation, no less. How she'd fallen into the pool but got out like she had expected it. She never seemed to miss a beat. She just kept persevering.

He could use some of that chutzpah, or whatever it was she had that kept her head up and shoulders back.

Gathering the extra scavenger-clue sheets and straightening the empty boxes waiting to receive food donations, he thought about how life had brought him here. His dad's illness brought him to Minier, Claire's plea got him to sign up to dress up as an elf, and Claire's broken leg brought Renee into his path.

He remembered his mom's favorite nighttime prayer when he was a little boy. "Lord, may we walk where you lead us, may we shoulder our daily burdens with grace and dignity, and may we always find our way back to what's right and good. Amen."

Maybe his mother's prayers had brought him to this moment.

If anything in his life was right and good right now, it was finding a new friend in Renee.

He just hoped it could lead to something more.

Chapter Thirteen

Seeing the sixth box of canned food donations filled Renee's heart with warmth. She was shocked to see her idea take flight so quickly. Maybe there was an upside to being out of corporate confinement: working in the community, for the community. Doing something in a small town required a couple of conversations, a plan, a presentation, and here they were, no months of requirements-gathering and approval before you could start doing the work.

It felt amazing.

But this elf costume was less than amazing. It was unusually warm for mid-December, and she could feel beads of sweat behind her knees under the flannel tights.

"Ugh. I need a shower," she said to Luke as they loaded the last box into his car. Only two boxes had fit in her car.

"Same. And this costume needs a spin in the washer."

"Better ask Mrs. White about that—not sure how well it would hold up. That thing is pretty old and has some mileage on it."

"Right." He shut the trunk and leaned against the car. "Hey, what are you doing tonight? I want to run to Bloomington and get pizza. Care to join me?"

"Yes, sounds good. I'll see if Claire wants to go with us."

Luke's eyebrows rose. "That would be great."

His tone didn't match his words, exactly. *Is he worried that Claire, on her crutches, would slow us down?*

"Where are we taking these boxes again?" Luke asked.

"To the maintenance building." Renee pointed west. "Follow me."

Securing the food in the designated space, they agreed to meet in front of Claire's building in an hour. Enough time to shower and change before going to town.

In the apartment, Claire was sitting on the couch, watching "National Lampoon's Christmas Vacation" and eating ramen noodles. Renee asked Claire if she wanted to go to town for pizza with her and Luke, but Claire snorted. "I'm not going to be the third wheel on your date."

"It's not a date!" How could her sister think that?

"Yeah, right!" Claire raised an eyebrow like a judge behind an enormous desk. "He asked you to dinner. It's Saturday night. Tell me that's not a date."

"He didn't say, 'Want to go on a date?'" Renee pulled off her elf shoes. "He said, 'Do you want to get pizza?'"

Claire shook her head. "There's some odd glitch in your brain that I'm not seeing. He asked you out. It's a date. Unless he said some very obvious disclaimer like, 'This isn't a date, but want to go get pizza?' or 'I'm just asking as a friend, want to get pizza?' Otherwise, it's a date."

"I think you're wrong."

"I'm right." She put the empty bowl on the coffee table, nudging aside a stack of reading material. "Admit it. When he tries to kiss you later, you owe me fifty bucks."

"I don't have a job. I'm broke, you know that."

"If you're so confident, you should take the bet. Easy money. But you know I'm right."

"Wouldn't it be weird if your friend and I dated?" She pulled off the Christmas bell earrings she wore with her costume and set them on the end table. "That's ick. Why didn't you two date?"

"We're just friends. Colleagues. For one, it would be uncomfortable dating someone I work with, and besides, I don't find him attractive."

"What?" Renee looked at Claire with obvious shock on her face. "Are you crazy?"

Claire beamed. "You do, then, don't ya?"

Renee thought of the pictures of Luke she'd taken earlier. The only thing wrong with them was the silly costume he had on. Everything else was perfect; he was the definition of male attractiveness. He looked like he could model for a men's fashion magazine. For once, she wished she were a people photographer.

Flustered, she grabbed a light sweatshirt and jeans out of her suitcase, along with clean underwear. She stomped into the bathroom, ready for a hot shower and an emotional reset.

Standing outside her sister's building forty minutes later waiting for Luke to arrive, Renee realized she didn't know where Luke lived. There was a lot she didn't know about him, and she planned to use their time together to find out more.

She glanced into the storefront window of the beauty shop, closed for the evening. The window had been decorated for the holidays with lights and festive window clings. On the front door was a flyer with all the Twelve Holly Days of Christmas activities listed. She smiled to read, "Santa's Elves will assist with all events!"

Crazy to think how just two weeks ago tonight, she was at her company's holiday party, feeling successful, leading the largest project of the year and gunning for her next promotion. And now, two short weeks later, she was job hunting and dressing up as an elf on the regular.

"Wild," she muttered to herself.

The sound of a car approaching caused her to turn, but it was a police cruiser, not Luke. She squinted at the officer inside, wondering if she knew them. *Nope.*

A few moments later, Luke pulled up to the curb in front of her. He parked and hopped out of his SUV.

"Is Claire coming?" he asked.

"No, she refused." Renee would not tell him why. "Just us."

"All right." He smiled. "Ready?"

He walked around the front of the car and opened the passenger door for her. *Was this a date?*

"Thank you," Renee said, climbing in.

She buckled her seatbelt. When he sat in the driver's seat, she said, "Nice ride. Kind of big for a bachelor. I think my Mini Cooper could fit in the back."

Luke laughed and glanced into the back of his SUV. "Perhaps. Don't forget I was a real estate agent." Luke put the car in reverse and backed out of the space. "Needed something big to cart my clients around in. Now it comes in handy for taking my dad to his appointments; sometimes he needs a wheelchair."

"Really?"

"Yes. He can walk, but there are days after chemo that he has zero energy. It's easier to use the wheelchair than to carry him." He laughed softly.

"Wow, that's really rough. Hey, where do you live? Can we drive by before leaving town?"

"You don't know where I live?" he asked.

"No."

"Oh, I thought Claire would have told you. Sure, we'll drive by."

He took a right at the next intersection, then another right; they were backtracking. Good thing it was a small town—it wouldn't take long to get there.

"How do you like living in Minier?" Renee asked. "It's pretty different from Springfield."

"It is, but I like it."

"Think you'll move back when your dad gets better?"

"Don't think so. I've enjoyed being closer to him. And I'm loving my role at the high school. It might not be what I aspired to before, but aspirations change. I'm mostly content."

His voice trailed off, and Renee thought about what he wasn't content with. Would it be too forward to ask?

"Here we are. Dad's place."

He parked in front of a two-story white house with a modest front porch big enough for a glider and two chairs.

Dark green shutters accented the windows, and the front door was a matching green. Three steps led to the porch.

"Nice," Renee said.

"It's good for him."

Renee nodded. "You mentioned a wheelchair. How do you manage those stairs?"

"Carefully." Luke chuckled. "You notice the details, don't you?"

"I try."

She loved to study buildings and structures, looking for interesting angles while framing a picture.

"Ready?"

"Sure. Which room is yours?" she asked.

"I have a small apartment at the back of the garage."

"You have an apartment in the garage? That's odd. Did you build it when you moved in?"

"No, it was there. A previous owner put it in. It's handy."

"But doesn't that add to your dad's electric and heating bills?"

"Yes, Miss Nosy, it does. But I pay the extra. No different than if I was renting something somewhere else. The cost is worth the privacy. I'm a grown adult. I don't want to be living under my dad's roof again."

"Ah, so you can take girls home and not get caught."

"It's not like that."

Luke turned onto Route 9, heading east to Bloomington. The corn and soybean fields were bare; some still contained stalk stumps, not yet plowed under.

He turned the radio volume up a few notches, so it was still soft enough for them to talk. A popular hit from the nineties was playing, and it made Renee smile.

"What's it like then?"

"What?"

"Your love life. Or dating life. Whatever they're calling it these days?" She shifted in her seat to get a better look at him.

Luke glanced at her, smiling. "'Whatever they're calling it these days'? Sounds like you don't do a lot of dating yourself."

She thought about her nonexistent dating life. There had been no one interesting enough in a long time. And after the debacle with her boss, maybe it was best if she stayed single until she was forty. By then she would likely find a man ready for his second wife, someone with alimony payments and kids in college.

But she wanted her own kids. Still, that didn't require marriage; she had other options.

"We're talking about you, not me," she replied, banishing thoughts of her calamitous relationship history from her mind.

"I've dated, but not since moving here. Small town and all. But no serious girlfriends to mention. I haven't found the right one, or maybe it wasn't the right time. Or I was too focused on work, I don't know."

He slowed at the stop sign.

Renee sighed. "Wow. Kind of similar to my situation. I'm too focused on work. No one serious. Bad timing." She thought about the impulsive kiss that had led to her being here now. "Bad decisions."

Luke grunted. "Same."

"So, you haven't fallen for anyone here?" An image of Alexis flashed through her mind. If she filed for divorce, she'd be a catch.

"No. Lots of great people here, but I've been focused on taking care of my dad."

"Maybe it's time to focus on you," she said. "Do you ever feel that biological clock? Like you should be married by thirty, have kids by thirty-five, own your own business by forty? That sort of thing?"

He chuckled. "Sometimes, yes. I'll be thirty next year, as a matter of fact. I think when those milestone birthdays loom, you think about where you are in life and where you're going. Self-assess. Are you where you want to be?"

"Yes, like an after-action review. We do them after every project at work. You ask the team, what were the expected outcomes? What were the actual outcomes? What can we do better next time? We could do that personally every year on our birthdays."

"We could." He paused. "You do, don't you?"

Renee laughed. "Maybe. Something like that, anyway."

"Ha, I knew it. I'd love to see your after-action review for dating. I could use a few pointers."

"Ready to get back in the game, huh?"

He turned towards her. "Yes."

A thrill shot through her. His eyes turned back to the road, but not before he'd seemed to connect with something in her soul.

That was good, right? Would she like to date Luke? He hadn't really asked her out, or had he? Was this a date?

He said he was ready to start dating, which must mean he wasn't considering this a date. So that was good.

But she wasn't staying; she was just here to fulfill her sister's role in the holiday festival. After Christmas, she would hopefully have a new job lined up and could afford to stay in her apartment. Otherwise, she would need to pack and move.

Now was not the time to consider dating someone 'back home'. That was a fun premise for a Hallmark movie, but it wasn't real life.

Time to change the subject. All this talk of dating was making Renee uncomfortable. She remembered the vision board she'd put together the day after college graduation. She'd checked off so many of the goals already—get a good job, pay off student debt, take a solo road trip from Chicago to New Orleans. But fall in love, marry before thirty, have her first baby by thirty-three—with a non-existent dating life, those were not looking good at this point.

At least, she had three years before reassessing at her thirtieth birthday milestone.

Maybe it was time for a new vision board. One that didn't include falling for a guy in Minier.

Chapter Fourteen

After the server took their order, Luke leaned back to rest against the high back of the booth. Fayet's Pizza had been around for at least thirty years. Renee remembered coming here during high school. It was a fun joint with loud music, cheap drinks, and hot pizza.

Luke asked, "Did you grow up in Minier?"

"Guilty as charged."

"A Minierian."

"Is that what we're called? Sounds too much like a minion."

"With the way some of the older generation clip their r's, I agree. So you must have lots of fond memories of the Holly Days festivities."

"Actually, they haven't been around that long. I think they started when I was entering high school, and I was too cool for it."

"High schoolers are so cool."

"As you'd know, counseling them and all. That must be a challenging job. I hope it's rewarding."

"It's good. I enjoy coaching and mentoring, helping them figure out their best path forward after high school. For some it's college, for others, trade school, for some military, and some need to care for family."

"Like you."

"Yeah, sort of like me. Though this is a recent development in my life, not something I had to do right out of high school."

"True." She leaned closer; she loved finding out more about Luke. "What made you decide to go into real estate?"

"I love looking at houses, thinking about possibilities. Where to place a game table, how to arrange the furniture in the family room for movie watching? Would the yard support a small garden or a firepit? And working with people has always been a sweet spot. After my first year of counseling, I thought I would never get my student loans paid off. So I thought, what else can I do to make cash? A friend was taking the realtor exam, and I thought I'd sign up."

"Were you good at it?"

"I was great at it. Top sales earner for my agency three years in a row."

"Why can't you do it here?"

"Minier's not big enough. I don't want to drive twenty to thirty minutes to a bigger town to make the money. A downside of real estate is that you're never truly off the clock. Clients can call at all hours of the day, wanting to see a house and make an offer. Now that I've been out of real estate for a while, I don't know that I would go back."

The server put their drinks down and walked away. A toddler a few tables away had a meltdown and flopped onto the floor, screaming. They both looked at the little boy and back at each other with raised eyebrows.

"Yikes," Renee said.

"Poor kid. Poor parents." Luke took a sip of his tea. "Now, what about you? You're job hunting. What are you looking for?"

"I'm desperate for anything right now. I hope to find another project management position with a large company, with good pay and room for promotions."

"In Chicago?"

"Ideally. But I'm open to moving. My lease is up February first, so logically, I could move anywhere."

"Oh?" His eyes widened, the green reminding her of a Christmas tree. "Would you consider moving back to Central Illinois?"

She scrunched her nose. "I don't think so. I like where I am, having access to everything the city offers—the museums, the restaurants, the sporting events."

"Do you go to sporting events?"

"Yes."

"And pay for overpriced concessions?"

"It can't be helped."

"But why? Do you love sports? Which team is your favorite?"

She looked away. "Whichever team is winning? I don't know. I don't care about sports, but it can be good for your career. I have to keep up with sports so I can join in the watercooler talk. Especially with the men, but the women usually follow local teams, too. It's an icebreaker."

"I bet you have lots of those."

Renee laughed. "I have books about icebreakers. A valuable tool for a project manager trying to lead a team."

"Give me an example."

"Two truths and a lie is a good one."

"Two truths and a lie?" His head tilted, questioning.

"Yes, you come up with three statements about yourself, and others have to guess which one is the lie."

"Let's do that. You start."

She smiled. "Fine. I've done this a few times. You ready?"

Luke nodded.

"Okay." She held up a finger. "One, I sang karaoke in a gay club on Bourbon Street. Two, I've had a picture published in the Chicago Tribune. Three, I was in a competitive theater group in high school."

"Oh wow. This is cool. All of them seem realistic and outrageous at the same time. This is going to be tough."

He looked up at the ceiling. "Hmm, I know you take photographs, so I think the Tribune could be true. Karaoke at a gay club sounds fun. Competitive theater seems far-fetched. I'll say three is the lie."

"No, that's true. The lie is the karaoke. I hate to sing in public."

"The details—the city, the type of bar—that made the lie plausible."

She smiled. "Now it's your turn. Two truths and a lie."

He smirked. "This is new to me. Give me a moment. I'm not one to stretch the truth. I don't know that I can lie."

Renee rolled her eyes. "Yeah, right! You sold real estate—you had to bend the truth at some point."

"No! Never! There's a professional oath."

She laughed. "All right. Come on. Let's hear them."

He paused and tapped a finger on his lip, drawing her attention to it.

He grinned. "Here goes. One, I love rock climbing. Two, I stole a car and took it for a joyride in high school. Three, I love to bake and dream of opening a bakery."

"All right. You came to play! None of them sound like the truth. Where would you rock climb in central Illinois? Bake? No way. Now, you made a cheesecake that you said was no-bake. Stole a car? Maybe as a reckless teenager." She paused. "I'm going to guess the lie is baking."

He grinned. "That's the truth, and I stole a car. I'm very ashamed to admit it. Luckily, my dad smoothed things over with the neighbor, and no charges were pressed. The lie is rock climbing. I've never done it."

"You bake? What? The muffins?" She tilted her head and raised an eyebrow.

"All me." He grinned.

"You said you bought them."

"Surprise!"

Renee chuckled. "They were to die for."

"Oh, I'm glad to hear that. Baking is my way to relax. I love trying new recipes and experimenting. It's a nice way to pretend I have some control over something when the world seems completely out of kenrol."

"Wow, poetic."

"Maybe."

The server arrived with the pizza, and Renee nearly drooled over the aroma of cheese, sausage and green pepper. Her stomach rumbled.

"Did you eat lunch?"

"A banana. I was so excited about the food drive that I was too nervous to eat."

"I'm not sure what you mean by that." Luke grabbed the handle of the pizza server and lifted. "Your plate?"

Renee lifted her plate, and he placed a perfectly browned slice on it.

"Yum," she said, placing a napkin in her lap. "So, a bakery, huh?"

"Yes, a dream. But like I said before, I don't want to drive twenty minutes away at three in the morning to bake, and I don't know that Minier can support a bakery."

Renee used her knife and fork to cut a bite-size piece of pizza.

"So, tell me more about your photography. Kudos for getting something in the Tribune."

"You changed the subject abruptly. We were talking about your bakery."

"We were talking about a dream. Now, tell me about the pictures, that's reality."

"It's just a hobby. Something I like to do on walks."

"Well, sure, lots of people take pictures on their phones when they walk. But you have real camera equipment that you've either been gifted or spent money on. Which is it?" He wasn't messing with a fork; he picked up his slice of pizza and took a bite.

"A mix of both. My parents bought me an SLR while I was in high school, for a photography class. They bought it at a pawnshop. They weren't sure how serious I would be about it. You know teenagers, they can be flighty."

Luke laughed, so she continued, "Anyway, it's like I caught a bug. I've never gone more than a couple of weeks without a photo walk."

"Do you share your photography?"

"With my family and friends?"

"Sure. With anyone. Obviously, you got a picture in the newspaper, so you shared it with someone."

"That's an interesting story. There was a bar fight that got out of hand. I happened to be walking by when these three men came tumbling out of the bar throwing punches. One guy had an arm wrapped around another man. It was crazy. I snapped away from a safe distance, and after it ended, a reporter came up to me and asked if I had any decent shots. He asked me to submit the best one. I went home and worked on it and submitted it. They used it."

"Did you get a photo credit?"

"Yeah. That was pretty cool."

"I bet. So, you don't normally share."

"No, it's for me. I have some of my favorite pictures hanging in my apartment."

"Will you try to take over for tomorrow's photographer?"

Sunday was Six Geese a-Laying, and rather than try to replicate that somehow with a fun activity, the organizers decided it would be a nice day to take pictures with Santa. There was a ten-dollar fee for the photo, with proceeds going to the county animal shelter. Participants would take home a goose ornament.

"Oh, no. I don't take portrait shots. Besides, we'll be busy getting the kiddos ready for the photos."

"Yes, Holly and Jolly, the helpful elves."

"Are you regretting volunteering?"

"Why would I regret it?"

"Well, you thought you'd be partnered with my sister, but you're stuck with me."

"Stuck is not the right word. I've enjoyed every minute of it."

"Especially when I fell into the pool, right?"

"No, that was awful. I'm so sorry that happened."

"Do you think she did it on purpose?"

"Alexis? No, why would she do that?"

"We have a history of trying to one-up each other. Competitive."

"Tell me more."

"Aren't you sick of getting to know me yet?" Renee finished her pizza and reached for the spatula to get another slice.

"Never. You're pretty fascinating, Holly-Renee. It's been fun getting to know you."

Renee leaned back and studied Luke's face. He was being honest. She'd had to develop her fib meter working on critical projects. It was better to know if someone was falling behind on their task, and sometimes people weren't honest about their status.

"Likewise, Jolly-Luke."

His eyes held her gaze, transmitting more than words could.

Chapter Fifteen

Caleb passed the bowl of mashed potatoes across the table to Claire, bypassing Renee.

"Hey," she said. "I'm sitting right here."

"It looked like CeCe was going to salivate if she didn't get the potatoes ASAP," Caleb retorted.

"Wow, it's beginning to feel like Christmas, David," their mother, Susan, said. "All the kids sitting around the table, fighting."

"It's almost like the good old days. We've sold our house, ready for our extended trip, and Caleb is hosting a family dinner for the first time. Other than that, just like Christmas," David replied, passing the bottle of wine to his wife.

"Not at all like Christmas," Claire said, scooping a large spoonful of mashed potatoes onto her plate. "It's still a week before the big day, and Renee is actually here."

"Lucky you," Renee said, taking the offered bowl and scooping her own potatoes. "Are you excited for your trip, Mom? Anything I can help you with before you go?"

"Right. You can't play Holly the elf twenty-four seven." Caleb sliced off a large piece of ham and plopped it on his plate.

"Thank goodness for small miracles." Though Renee enjoyed the time spent as Holly, she needed to make progress with the job hunt.

"I want to go shopping this week for some last-minute items, and I have a little Christmas shopping to finish. Would love your company."

"Of course. I have a few phone interviews this week." *Finally!* "And holidates merriment in the evenings. Would love to shop with you."

Renee thought about her dwindling checking account. Good thing she'd bought most of her family's gifts before Thanksgiving. Planning ahead for the win!

"It's going to be weird celebrating Christmas here," Claire said, glancing around Caleb's functional but plain dining room.

"Hey, I'll decorate," Caleb said. "It'll be festive."

"Maybe Renee could help with that while you're working," David said.

Great, now I'm everyone's personal assistant. An unpaid personal assistant.

"Oh, sweet. That would be so helpful!" Caleb said, putting his hand on Renee's shoulder and squeezing. "The decorations are in the crawl space. I'll give you a key before you go. Come over anytime."

Renee rolled her eyes. Great, another task for her to-do list. "How's the little pantry cabinet coming along, little brother?" Renee asked.

"Easy-peasy. It'll be done on Tuesday. Is the location solid?"

"Yes, the village signed off on the space outside of the town hall. Will you need help moving it and setting it up?"

"With your scrawny muscles?" Caleb pulled back from her and scoffed. "No thanks. It's heavy."

"Maybe Luke could help," Renee suggested.

"Right. Renee's new boyfriend," Claire said, smirking.

"Not my boyfriend." *But if the timing were different.*

"What about a boy?" Susan asked.

"Not a boy; Luke's a grown man."

"Well!" Susan smiled at David, "Sounds like there's a young man in Renee's life. Things are getting exciting, and we're leaving for an extended trip. Drats."

"Things are not exciting. He's just my festivities co-host, nothing more. Besides, I should be out of town right after Christmas myself. No need to stick around after Christmas; the twelve magical days of Minier will be over then."

"But your sister could still use your help!" Susan protested as she poured more wine into her glass.

"Ha!" Renee said. "She's an athlete who could run circles around me on those crutches. She doesn't really need my help."

"Carrying groceries up the stairs on the crutches is a pain in my—"

"Claire," David warned.

"Sorry, Dad, neck. Pain in my neck."

"Still no grocery delivery in town?" Renee asked.

"Of course not. Your big-city conveniences didn't follow you home."

"Shame."

There were so many things she took for granted, living in Chicago. There were probably lots of residents who would benefit from delivery services here. Maybe she should talk to the mayor about options.

"What's everyone looking forward to this week?" Susan inquired, diverting the conversation back to neutral ground.

Claire tossed her hand up to go first. "School break officially begins at 3:10 PM on Friday. Two weeks off."

"I'm looking forward to finishing the cabinet for the food pantry. It's going to help a lot of people." Caleb patted Renee's back. "Proud of you, sis, for coming up with the idea and getting approval from the town."

Renee felt her cheeks flush. "And thank you for creating the actual pantry. It's going to be great."

"Yes, Renee." Her dad lifted his glass of wine. "Well done."

"You'll be running for political office before we know it," Susan said.

"No way." Renee thought back to the humiliation of losing the prom court vote. *Not subjecting myself to any sort of voting outcome again.* Though, in a way, job applications were a sort of vote, weren't they? At least she didn't have to see her competitors.

"What are you looking forward to this week, Renee?" Claire asked.

"Um, besides Christmas?" Everyone chuckled. "Probably the Santa Parade on Saturday. I'll be able to hang up the elf costume after that."

"But your mandatory time with Luke will be over then," Claire said.

Renee ignored the comment. "What are you looking forward to, Mom?"

"Filling your stockings on Christmas Eve."

"Dad?"

"Work presentation on Thursday. We've been working on it for a few weeks. I'll be able to relax once we get approval."

"And then you retire one week later. Amazing," Caleb said.

The conversation turned towards the parents' upcoming trip.

Renee listened and chimed in appropriately, but her mind kept wandering to Luke. He'd been so adorable earlier at the pictures with Santa event, helping the little kids get up on Santa's lap and encouraging them to smile for the camera. He'd had to calm a few screamers but handled all the stress with ease.

The more she interacted with him and got to know him, the more difficult it was to imagine the end of their time working together on the holiday festivals.

It was even harder to think about going back to her lonely apartment in Chicago. Sleeping on her sister's couch wasn't the most comfortable, and she regretted the limited wardrobe she'd brought with her but getting to see her sister every day was a remedy she hadn't known she needed. The evening conversations, sitting on the couch with cups of herbal tea and talking about their day, were comforting. Claire asked about the festival events and Renee's job search progress. And Renee asked about the kids and teachers at school.

They found it funny that they each got to see Luke every day, Claire in his normal clothes and Renee in the elf costume. After she'd returned from dinner with Luke the night before, Claire had asked Renee if her feelings for him were changing, and though she knew they were, she wasn't ready to share her growing attraction to Luke.

She didn't see a future with him, and there was no sense in confessing her feelings without the possibility of something happening between them. At the end of this week, she hoped Luke would consider her a friend, and that would have to be good enough.

Monday night's activity, watching the movie "The Swan Princess" at the library, was uneventful. The kids behaved well, the movie played with no technical issues, and the popcorn machine popped plenty of popcorn.

At the end of the night, Luke had said to Renee, "We put costumes on for this?"

Renee had two Zoom interviews on Tuesday morning; neither job seemed a good fit for her. One was in Cincinnati, and the other was a project-manager supervisor role, which didn't sound that appealing.

After the interviews, she submitted online applications for five more jobs. *Here's hoping things go my way soon.*

Caleb sent her a text message at noon, saying he finished the food pantry and they needed a plan to deliver it and put it in place.

She called the mayor and asked if he wanted any special announcements, a ribbon cutting, or any other formalities, but he said not to delay it. He knew they had food ready to put in it, and he wanted it available as soon as they could get it going. He suggested she call the social media manager to get a few pictures and posts ready to go, and apparently, Alexis was the social media manager. Easy enough.

Twenty minutes later, she had a plan to meet Caleb, Luke, and Alexis outside the town hall at four o'clock. She would borrow her parents' truck to get all the food out of storage.

I love it when a plan comes together.

One more thing would take this over the top. She picked up her phone to text Luke again.

RENEE: How about wearing our elf costumes for the food pantry setup? Alexis will take pictures for social media.

She didn't have to wait long.

LUKE: Love the idea. Can we make it 4:15?

RENEE: Yes. I'll let the others know.

Chapter Sixteen

Renee watched as Luke and Caleb hoisted the large cabinet that would serve as the free pantry off Caleb's delivery truck, using arm straps, patience, and a little sweat.

Alexis snapped several pictures of Caleb in action, but not of Luke. She said she didn't want to disillusion kids by showing Jolly the Elf delivering the pantry. She thought it would be better to have pictures of the elves loading the pantry with food.

"Whatever you prefer," Renee said. Alexis was the social media manager, and Renee was done stepping on the woman's toes.

"This is so exciting," Alexis said. "I can't wait until the message gets out about this, Renee. It's a great idea. I'm sorry I didn't see it at first. I think it was all the stress."

"Hey, no worries. I'm sorry I went around you. I can be a little hardheaded when I get a hold of an idea."

Luke and Caleb reached the spot that was the new home of the pantry and shimmied it into place.

Alexis slid her phone into her back pocket and clapped her hands. "This is so exciting!"

Renee smiled, snapping a few photos of her brother and Luke with her phone, wishing she'd remembered her SLR camera.

"How does this look?" Caleb called, giving his side of the cabinet a little push.

"Perfect. Can we load it up?"

Caleb walked to his truck and picked up a toolbox. "Hold on for a couple of minutes. I'm going to drill bolt holes through it to secure it to the building. Not taking any chances of it toppling over on someone."

"Wow, smart," Luke said, unwrapping the lifting straps from his arms and tossing them in the back of Caleb's delivery van.

"We can bring the boxes out while he does that," Renee said, walking towards the borrowed truck.

Alexis pulled her phone out but paused with a hand on her hip. "Hmm, I don't think a picture of you guys unloading from a regular vehicle makes sense. I'll wait for you to finish unloading."

"You could grab a box, couldn't you?" Renee asked.

"Oh, duh. Yes." She put her phone away again and grabbed the closest box.

Fifteen minutes later, the pantry was bolted to the wall behind it, the boxes were unloaded, and Alexis had taken countless photos of Holly and Jolly stocking the pantry.

"Well, are our happy elves ready for tonight's event?" Alexis asked as they walked towards their cars.

"No!" Luke groaned.

"Oh, I don't know," Renee teased. "I'm hoping we can get you to milk a cow."

"I'll be ready to take pictures," Alexis said.

"I can't imagine that will happen." Luke shook his head emphatically.

Tonight was the Eight Maids a-Milking activity. A cow-milking contest was held at the high school, hosted by the local Future Farmers of America organization. The competition allowed everyone to take part. It was a popular activity, and the entry fees went into a scholarship program for the FFA students.

"Never say never," Alexis called over her shoulder as she climbed into her car.

Luke looked at Renee. "Ever feel all dressed up and nowhere to go?"

They had three hours before the evening's event, and they were in their costumes. "Yes. Should we just go change and meet up tonight?" She could use the time to talk to Claire about what she needed from town. Renee and their mom were planning to shop on Wednesday.

"I have a better idea," Luke said. "Come with me."

Luke drove to Mackinaw and parked in front of the small regional hospital. He turned to Renee and pointed to the back seat, where a large basket of candy canes sat.

"Why don't we go in and hand out candy canes and cheer up the patients?" His intense green eyes flashed with excitement.

"Oh, Luke. That's sweet."

"Great. Come on. My dad is a regular visitor, so I know a bunch of the staff."

He exited the car and opened the door to the back seat as Renee walked around the vehicle.

"Your dad gets treatment here?" Renee asked as she straightened her elf costume.

"Yes, he had to go to Peoria for surgery, but treatments are here."

They walked towards the entrance. The wind was blowing briskly, and Luke knew it would be chilly once the sun went down. The weather forecaster said there could be snow this week. *It would be great to have a white Christmas.*

Entering the building, Luke motioned for Renee to turn to the right. The receptionist at the information desk stood and shrieked when she saw him in his costume.

"What do we have here? An elf?" Leaning toward him, she said, "Is that you, Luke?"

"Hi, Monique. Yes, it's me." He pointed to his name tag. "Jolly."

"Well, I'll call you Jolly and you can call me Happy. It's good to see you, Jolly." She gave him a wink and a quick hug. "How's your daddy doing?"

"He's stringing a few good days together, so good. We'll take it."

"That's great, sweetie. Who's your friend?" she asked, turning to Renee.

Luke leaned forward and whispered, "Renee." Then in a loud voice he said, "Holly." Turning to Renee, he said. "This wonderful woman is Miss Monique. She's amazing."

"Pleasure to meet you, Miss Holly," Monique said. "It's not every day we get Santa's helpers walking in here."

"Pleasure's mine," Renee said.

"Looks like you two are on a mission," Monique said, looking at the basket in Luke's hands.

"We are. Here to spread some cheer," he said. "Do we need guest passes?"

"In those getups? No, dear. I'll send a text blast to the staff letting them know what you're doing. You're pretty easy to identify, so don't cause any trouble."

"I'd never consider it, Monique. Thank you," Luke said.

It took a little over an hour to walk the halls, say hello to patients, and take pictures when patients and staff requested them.

Returning to Luke's car, he tossed the empty basket into the backseat. "Should we head straight to the high school now? It'll take thirty minutes to get there. Do you need to stop at your car or Claire's place to get anything?"

Renee shook her head, and Luke backed out of the parking space. "That was fun. Great idea, to visit the hospital."

"Thanks. A teacher brought me the basket of candy canes today and asked if I could use them. She'd ordered them for her classes, but there was a shipping error, and she got a double order. The company didn't want them back. So anyway, that was fun!"

From the corner of his eye, Luke watched Renee open her tote bag and pull out a planner. She flipped a few pages until she reached a calendar. She opened her phone and began scrolling with a pen in hand. He was itching to look at her calendar, but he had to keep his eyes on the road.

Maybe he should ask her out again. The next week was packed with festival activities, followed closely by

Christmas. The twelfth and last day of the festival was on Saturday, with a Santa parade followed by a talent contest, which would hopefully feature some drummers drumming.

Renee had said she was leaving after Christmas, but would she really? No time like the present to find out.

"How's your calendar look?" Luke asked. "I bet I can guess what you're doing every night this week."

"Oh, that's funny. You can. I'm trying to schedule interviews for next week. Got two requests while we were busy this afternoon."

"Great." He said the word but didn't feel the sentiment. "What day are you looking at?"

"Next Wednesday, I hope."

"Wednesday? My dad goes in for a full-body scan. A cancer check."

She put her phone down and turned to him. "Really? I hope that goes well."

"Thanks. I do, too. And of course, I hope the interviews go well for you."

"Thanks."

She scribbled on her calendar, and Luke let the conversation lapse.

She had a life far from here. She'd only promised to stay to help her sister out. There was nothing to keep her here after the holiday.

When it looked like she'd finished making notes, Luke asked, "What are your plans the day after Christmas? Tuesday? I think we should do something fun to celebrate the end of the festival elfin duties. I'll be on Christmas break from school, and if you're around, maybe we can go get breakfast. Or hit the after-Christmas sales."

"You dare to go into the stores the day after Christmas?"

"I love a bargain," Luke admitted. *And I would do anything to spend more time with you.*

"You are full of surprises, Luke Woods. Sure, if I'm still here, that would be great. We should commemorate the end of this project."

"Maybe we can even do an after-action review," Luke suggested, remembering Renee's conversation about her job.

Renee laughed, that deep, from the chest laugh that he'd heard only a few times. It was her genuine laugh, not the forced laugh she gave when it was expected. He'd learned the difference.

"Oh, Luke, you know I've started a list."

He smiled. He wasn't surprised by her statement.

Chapter Seventeen

Renee's mom, Susan, pointed to the right. "Turn here."

Pulling into the In Bloom flower shop, Renee parked next to the building and admired its colorful mural depicting a variety of pretty flowers. In front of the building were large pots of poinsettias, three-foot tall evergreen trees decorated with ornaments and bows, and several pots filled with birch logs tied with plaid ribbons. "Cute place."

"I love stopping in here. The ladies are so nice," Susan said, climbing out of Renee's compact car. "Unfortunately, we don't have a lot of room, so I'll have to watch what I buy."

Renee closed her door and glanced in the back window. They'd put the backseat down for more room, but their purchases nearly overflowed the space.

"Good thing this is the last stop," Renee said, checking her watch.

Inside the store, pine, cinnamon, and rose scents wafted over them. Decorative floral arrangements and holiday gifts lined every shelf and table. Several shoppers were milling around, and two women with matching aprons were answering questions.

Susan ooh-ed and ah-ed over several arrangements before finding a tall vase that looked like a birch tree stump filled with evergreen branches, pinecones and white roses. "This would look great in Caleb's dining room, don't you think?"

"Yeah, festive and masculine. I think it'll work well."

Renee looked around for an arrangement for Claire's kitchen. She chose one with soft green foliage, white hydrangeas, and juniper stems with blue berries.

"Oh, that's lovely," Renee said. "Anything else?"

Renee shook her head. "If we buy anything else, we'll have to strap it to the roof of my car."

"You're right. Let's check out."

"Hello." The woman behind the counter, whose nametag read "Tilly", looked about the same age as Renee. "Did you find what you needed?"

"Yes, we did. We'd probably buy more, but we're in a packed tiny car," Susan said, setting her vase on the counter. "I'll get that one, too."

"No, I'm getting this," Renee protested. "It's a hostess gift for Claire, for putting up with me."

Susan smiled. "Oh, that's lovely, dear."

Tilly rang up their purchases, and they left. At the car, Susan put one arrangement on the floor between her feet and set the other one on her lap. "Please watch out for potholes, or water will splash on my lap and shoes."

Renee navigated out of the parking lot, and soon they were heading west towards Minier.

"That was a productive shopping trip, and I'll have time to shower and get ready before I have to be at tonight's event."

"What's tonight's event?"

"Nine Ladies Dancing, so we're watching the movie 'White Christmas'. I'm surprised they went for such an old movie, but I didn't design the activities, I just play Holly."

"At least you have a very handsome Jolly," Susan said before being racked with a sneeze.

"Bless you. Too many fresh flowers, huh? There's tissue in the glove box if you need it."

"Thanks." Susan reached for a tissue. "That sounds fun. A movie night must be easy for you, at least."

"It is. But I don't know that they really need elves. Luke and I discussed that on Monday."

"How is it working with Luke?"

"Great. He's tolerable, I guess."

"Tolerable, huh? Think you could be more than just partners in elf costumes?"

"Nooo." Renee dragged the word out like it was obvious. "We live three hours apart. Won't work."

Susan shifted, tilting the flowers in her lap away from her face. "Well, you are job hunting. What's keeping you from looking here? There's Bloomington. Peoria and Champaign are not very far. You said your lease is up soon; you could move."

"I don't think I'll find a job paying as much as I could earn in the city." Renee slowed to make a turn.

"Life's not always about how much you can make," Susan stressed. "What you earn doesn't define you. At least it shouldn't. We only get one life, Renee, so make the most of it. Don't chase promotions and paychecks until you're too old to enjoy life. You'll eventually see that a job won't cheer you up when you're sick, or comfort you when you're sad. Jobs won't be there to hold your hand at the end of your life. People will. Surround yourself with people who love you, not just those competing against you for the next promotion."

She sighed. "Look at your dad and me. All those years putting off big vacations because we were raising you kids. Now, here we are after your dad's retirement, taking a six-month cruise all around the world. I just hope nothing big happens while we're gone, like one of you getting engaged."

"Mom," Renee started, but stopped, letting her mom's words sink in. It was a valid point. Maybe it was time to prioritize relationships over work. But she needed money in order to eat and have a place to live, so she needed a job. Maybe she didn't have to be as rigid in her job requirements, though. Maybe extending her search wasn't a bad idea.

Taking a deep breath, Renee nodded. "Okay, I hear you. Sound advice."

She changed the subject to talk about the Christmas menu. Neither of them was confident that Caleb would put the turkey in the oven on time.

"I'll text him," Renee said.

"That's my girl. You'll bring dessert, right?"

That made Renee think about the cheesecake Luke had made and his dream of opening a bakery. She admired his willingness to change career direction, leaving real estate to become a counselor and considering opening a bakery.

He didn't see himself as his job. He was bigger than his job; he was a caring son, community member, and friend. Those were his priorities. He had a way of trusting that things were going to be all right, even if they didn't go as he'd planned.

Renee knew there was plenty she could learn from him. Leaving next week was not going to be easy.

Luke stepped into the grade-school gym and saw Alexis at the check-in table. The bells on his jacket jingled as he brushed through the doorway.

"Hi, Jolly," she called as he approached.

"Alexis. Anything I can do to help set up?"

"No, everything's ready. Just greet people as they come in. Is Holly coming?"

"For certain. I'm sure she'll be here soon. Expecting a lot of people?"

"Not sure. It's the first year we've shown this movie. Hope it's popular."

"Same." He leaned against the wall. "Hey, I saw the social media post earlier. Asking for food donations instead of a ticket fee was a great idea. The pantry should stay stocked through the holidays."

Her eyes lit up. "Good to know you saw it. Sometimes I think the algorithm buries all the town posts; the engagement is low."

"Oh, I'll remember to share them when I see them. Not that I have a lot of engagement, but I'm sure it helps."

Alexis tossed her long hair over her shoulder. "It does."

The door opened, and a gust of cold air rushed in. A group of people wrapped in heavy coats followed. Everyone carried a canned good.

Luke looked at Alexis. "You might not get any money tonight."

She laughed and stood to greet the new arrivals.

As they filed into the gym, Renee walked in. "Brr, when did the temperature drop? Hi, Alexis. Jolly."

"Hey, Holly." Alexis pointed to the box for food donations. "Did you see the post about bringing food instead of paying for tonight?"

Renee's eyes widened, and her face lit up. Luke loved seeing her beam like that.

"No, I didn't! That's great. Posted it on social?" Renee pulled her phone out of her pocket and began scrolling.

"Yes," Alexis answered. "The idea just came to me a few hours ago."

"You didn't have to run it by the committee?" Renee asked.

Luke braced for fireworks.

Alexis looked chagrined. "No. Seemed like a no-brainer. Sometimes you have to ask for forgiveness instead of permission."

Renee smiled. "Amen to that." She held up her fist for a fist bump. Alexis laughed and complied.

Thirty minutes later, the bleachers were full, the lights dimmed, and the movie began.

Alexis asked Luke and Renee for help loading the boxes of canned goods into her car. When they'd finished, she said she had to leave to pick up Easton at her mother's house so they could go home for dinner.

"Night, Alexis," Renee and Luke chorused.

"I'm freezing!" Renee rushed toward the door.

Inside the building, Luke touched Renee's elbow. "Are you interested in the movie?"

"Not really. I've seen it before. We're all dreaming of a white Christmas, Bing."

Luke laughed. "My sentiments. Want to hang out in the office?" He pointed to the window next to them.

"Sure."

Luke grabbed a bag of popcorn from the foyer. In the office, they each took one of the leather club chairs. *This must be the VIP waiting area.*

He offered popcorn to Renee, but she waved it off. "I'm stuffed."

"How was your day? Any interviews?"

Renee swiveled in her chair, swinging left to right, full of energy. "No. I went to Bloomington with Mom to shop."

"Nice. Finish your Christmas shopping?"

"Yeah, we're a pretty simple family. One gift each, limit twenty bucks. Our parents break that rule, but I guess they're allowed."

"Nice."

Luke needed to step up his conversational game; this was boring.

"So, did you think any more about breakfast after Christmas?"

She frowned slightly. "If I don't have any interviews lined up. I'm sorry to be noncommittal. I hope it's okay, even if it's a last-minute decision. Besides, I think Claire is eager to get rid of me before her Christmas break. She's not so subtle with the hints."

Luke laughed. "She's a straight shooter. If you had to, couldn't you stay with your brother?"

Renee rolled her eyes and dropped her head back onto the chair. The elf hat slipped off her head and landed on the floor. "Ugh. If I were desperate, maybe. Hopefully, it doesn't come to that. I've submitted a lot of resumés, so hopefully it picks up soon. Besides, it will be better if I'm at home, which gives me the flexibility for last-minute interviews. So, in answer to your question, the day after Christmas is probably not good to plan on."

Luke felt his heart sink. She was blowing him off and determined to stay in Chicago. Obviously, she was not that interested in him.

She shot forward. "What about Christmas Eve morning? Do you have plans with your dad? We don't have any."

As easily as his heart had sunk, it now soared.

"That would work, and it's after our last official act as Santa's elves: a true celebration."

"Yes, the light at the end of the candy cane tunnel."

Luke laughed. "Should I bring my notes for our after-action review?"

Renee's mouth twisted as she considered the question. "No, let's not. I'm sure Alexis will have a committee meeting, and I'm sure you can give them my feedback."

"Wow. You trust me with that?"

"Yeah." She looked away, her eyebrows knitted together.

"You all right?"

"Yes. Just overthinking."

"Want to talk about it?" Luke leaned forward and put his hands up, wanting to appear open to listening.

She sighed. "Sometimes I can be a little much. High expectations for myself, high expectations for others, and I can be pushy. I want to work on that."

"Does that have something to do with you leaving your last job?"

She put her hands over her face and leaned back again. "I wish."

"Hey." Luke leaned toward her and put a hand on her knee. "If you want to talk about it, I'm here."

She took a few moments, dropped her hands and looked at him. "I made a really stupid, impulsive mistake, which made my boss uncomfortable, so he asked me to move to another team. I realized how stupid and damaging my mistake was, and I quit. My job performance was top-notch; it was an out-of-the-office issue."

Luke's mind was churning. *What could she have done to make her boss uncomfortable outside of work?* "Wow. My mind is all over the place. That was vague enough to be alarming."

The corner of Renee's lips tilted up. "It's the mistletoe's fault."

Luke shook his head. "You kissed him?"

"Yes. I blame the mistletoe."

"Wow. You do get into the holiday spirit, don't you?"

"Ha." She smiled, but it didn't reach her eyes. "Like I said, it was the mistletoe's fault. And maybe the punch was spiked."

"Isn't the punch always spiked?"

"Yes. I should have known. Anyway, to make matters even worse, turns out he's married. I worked for the man for two years, and it had never come up. I was mortified, absolutely mortified. I bolted."

She swung in her chair, faced the window, and shrugged. "Ask anyone around here. I'm a runner. Things get tough, and I run."

"No way." Luke shook his head. "I don't believe that. You are one of the toughest people I know."

"I'm not tough. I just plow forward. Don't admit defeat. Try, try again. I think project managers have to be that way. But I can't tell you how many times I went home at the end of a tough day and just bawled my eyes out. The stress can be intense."

"Then don't do it. You shouldn't be doing something that stresses you out like that. It'll kill you."

"Hmm, interesting. Similar advice from my mom today."

"I knew I liked your mom."

He wanted to tell Renee how much he liked her, but he refrained. She was dealing with a lot of work baggage tonight. He'd wait until she was in a better place mentally.

Since she'd opened up to him, he felt like things were moving in the right direction. And she'd agreed to breakfast. On Christmas Eve. How fitting, these two elves would have Christmas Eve off while the rest of Santa's elves would ready his sleigh.

This was not the event Luke wanted to attend without Renee. Ten Lords a-Leaping night was a community dance at the grade-school gym, with a long jump competition for good measure. *Those lords gotta leap!*

Three hours of too-loud music, distracted parents, and hyper kids, and Luke was ready to retreat to his tiny garage apartment and fall into bed with a book.

Alexis approached him with a smile and a crooked elf hat. She'd stood in for Renee tonight as Holly. He laughed when he saw her changes to Renee's costume; she'd replaced Renee's loose red belt with a large black belt like Santa would wear. He wasn't sure if she was trying to highlight the smallness of her waist or what, but it was a little silly. Or maybe he was just irritated.

"Jolly," Alexis called, "we need to present the long jump trophies to the winners." She waved for him to approach the table where the trophies sat. Male and female winners in four different age categories would get a trophy. The trophies didn't look like athletic long jumpers; they looked like lords a-leaping, and Luke could not figure out why anyone wanted to win one.

"I have the list of winners," Alexis continued. "I'll announce them if you'll hand out the trophies."

"Are we shaking hands, taking pictures, or what?"

"Mrs. White is taking the pictures, so follow her lead."

Luke felt like he was going through the motions. Stand with trophy, shake hands, smile for the camera. Repeat seven more times.

Renee's text message had been brief. "Can't make it tonight, have to run to Chicago for an important interview. Asked Alexis to fill in."

He'd been optimistic after their talk the night before. Renee had seemed contemplative, and he thought that meant she was ready for big changes in her life. Maybe leaving Chicago, finding an alternative career path. He wanted that for her, less stress, less hustle, less grind. And he hoped for a chance for them.

Arriving home, he was glad to see his dad's house was dark. He'd been bummed all night and didn't have the energy to be brave and cheerful for anyone, even himself.

He showered and crawled into bed, knowing tomorrow had to be a better day.

Chapter Eighteen

The townwide Christmas caroling extravaganza, otherwise known as Eleven Pipers Piping, kicked off from the library.

Renee looked around at everyone gathered. There were families, individuals, and couples in attendance. Alexis was counting heads to determine how to break everyone into small groups for caroling. All those who wanted to sing would be divided into groups and given a list of homes to visit, along with lyric sheets for the three or four songs in their rotation.

Luke approached from the parking lot, fully decked out in his elf costume. Renee still wished she could spend more time with him outside of the town Christmas festivities. He looked so much better in his casual quarter-zip shirts and sweatshirts than in the green elf suit, though the green of the suit highlighted his green eyes to perfection.

Approaching, Luke held out a stainless-steel cup. "Here, I brought you hot chocolate, with a hint of mint."

"Is this spiked?" she asked, sniffing the container.

"Maybe."

"I hope we don't end up under any mistletoe tonight."

Luke wiggled his eyebrows. "I hear strange things might happen."

She knew he was kidding, but his words made a shiver run down her shoulders. If she kissed him under the mistletoe, it would sure help dull the memory of kissing her boss. She assumed that she and Luke—the elves—would be assigned to different groups, so the chances were slim, but it was nice to think about.

"Excited about caroling tonight?" Luke asked.

"Caroling in a group where my lip-syncing doesn't get noticed? Not a problem. I told you—singing in public? Can't stand it."

"Yeah, you said that, but I thought you could do anything."

"No, far from it. I know what I'm good at, and I push myself to improve. And I know what I'm not good at, and stay far away from it. Singing is in the latter bucket."

"It's good when we know our limitations." Luke winked at her, and she felt her cheeks flush, thankful that the color could be assumed to be caused by the cold temperature and not embarrassment.

"All right!" Alexis called. "All right." The crowd chatter softened to a low murmur. "We're going to count off in sixes. Unless you have a group of five or six, let's say a family, that you want to stick together, just separate yourselves along the sidewalk. I'll help everyone count off to make our groups."

"Uh oh," Luke said. "I think she's going to separate some couples with that method, so we'd better keep a close eye on things to make sure no fights break out."

"You got it, Jolly," Renee said.

Once Alexis got everyone assigned, she asked Renee and Luke to join her small group, as she had a list of special houses to visit—shut-ins, an older gentleman from her church on hospice care, and a home with a recently placed foster child who was extremely anxious in his new surroundings. She thought these people would benefit from seeing the two elves.

Singing (or lip-syncing in Renee's case) at each house, Renee and Luke stood on either side of their small group. Renee always stood close to Alexis, who had a beautiful voice and wasn't afraid to sing out.

Walking from one house to the next, Luke and Renee would often fall back to talk, but nowhere on the walk did they end up under any mistletoe.

Once Alexis said they'd hit all the houses on her list, Luke asked her if they could swing by his dad's place.

Renee was excited that she was finally going to meet Luke's dad.

Approaching the house, Luke jogged ahead and walked in the front door. It took a few moments for him to reappear on the doorstep with Mr. Woods, who was wearing a heavy flannel jacket and a stocking cap.

"Everyone, this is my dad, Michael Woods." Luke turned to the carolers. "Dad, this is everyone!"

Their small group called out hellos and Christmas wishes before Alexis blew her pitch pipe and they launched into a rousing rendition of "Joy to the World".

Renee was at the back of the group and knew that the person in front of her wore thick earmuffs, so she actually joined in singing the chorus. Quietly, of course.

After their three songs, Mr. Woods went back inside, and Luke tugged on Renee's arm. "Want to stay and meet my dad?"

"Sure, I'd love to."

They said good night to the rest of the carolers before entering the house.

Luke led her through the kitchen and bare dining room to the living room.

Mr. Woods started to stand when they approached the couch.

"Please don't get up," Renee said, holding out her hand to the man.

"Fine. Nice to meet you, Renee," he said, shaking her hand. "Luke's told me a lot about you."

"Uh oh." Renee shook her head. "I hope it's not all bad, Mr. Woods."

He shook his head. "Please call me Michael. And he's said nothing bad. All positive." He glanced at Luke. "I think he's smitten with ya."

Luke groaned. "Dad." He shook his head. "I knew this was a bad idea."

Renee beamed.

Micheal began to cough.

"Are you okay?" Luke asked.

"Little too much fresh air," Michael answered. "Would you mind getting me some hot tea?"

"Be right back." Luke walked towards the kitchen.

Renee looked around the room and saw several photos of Luke's family on the wall. "Oh, how sweet," she said, approaching the pictures. There were the typical school photos and several of the family together. And in one, a very young Luke sat next to his mom, his brows furrowed in concentration, a partially finished gingerbread house in front of them. "Luke looks like his mother."

"Thank God," Michael said, laughing.

Renee smiled at him. "I think he's got your sense of humor, though."

"You got that right. He's a good man. Full of heart and laughter. Considerate."

"I see that."

"Good."

Luke entered the room with a large mug that smelled like Christmas, with hints of cinnamon, vanilla, and orange peel.

"Here you go, old man." Luke handed him the cup. "We'd better go before you embarrass me any further."

"Pleasure to meet you, Michael." Renee leaned over and gave him a quick hug.

"Pleasure's mine." He reached for the mug and pulled a TV tray closer.

Outside, Renee asked Luke about the lack of a kitchen or dining table.

"Funny that you ask that now. He just mentioned that he's thinking about getting one; he hasn't had one since shortly after Mom died. Said it was too painful to see it and not have her sitting at it. When he moved here, he sold the one he had and didn't want it replaced. I've been suggesting inviting family over, and he's softening."

"Wow. That's sad and sweet at the same time. I can't imagine losing the one you love."

"It's never easy. We all deal with grief in our own ways. I'm not pushing it, but I'm glad to hear he's open to the idea. Too bad I already got his gift." Luke laughed. "His birthday is in March, though."

"There you go."

Back at the library parking lot, cold and ready for a hot shower, Renee handed Luke the empty beverage container. "Thanks for the hot drink. I don't think I'd have made it to the end of the night without it."

"It wasn't too spiked?" Luke covered her hand with his before taking the cup, and Renee wished for a moment that they weren't wearing gloves, and that there'd been some mistletoe hanging along the route.

"No."

"Good." Luke glanced down the block towards Claire's apartment building. "Get in and get warm."

Renee walked towards her sister's building. Turning back, she said. "Good night, Luke."

"Night, Renee."

Before he got in the car, Renee said, "Hey, we're baking cookies tomorrow morning for Christmas. Want to join us?"

"At Claire's?"

"Yes."

"What time?"

"Nine."

"I'll be there."

"Great. See you tomorrow."

Maybe Renee could snap a few pictures of Luke wearing regular clothes tomorrow. She was going to need a few pictures of him when this weekend was over, and she returned to Chicago. Alone.

Walking into Claire's apartment the next morning, Luke's nose filled with his favorite smells—cinnamon, vanilla, and baked sugar.

Renee led him into the kitchen, where every inch of counter space held cooling racks packed with baked sugar cookies in snowman, tree, mitten, snowflake, and deer shapes. Several racks held gingerbread boy and girl cookies.

"I thought we were baking," Luke said, pulling his coat off.

"Not enough time," Renee said, taking his coat to put in the living room. "We realized we needed to get up super early this morning to bake, so we can get them decorated before we leave for the Santa parade."

"We're decorating the cookies?" Luke asked. "I'll warn you now, I'm better at baking than decorating."

Claire looked up from the blue snowflake she was decorating with tiny silver sugar balls. "Too bad, so sad, stud. Grab a piping bag."

Renee laughed at the banter between the two friends. "Do you two call each other pet names at work?"

"Absolutely not," Claire said.

"Well," Luke said sheepishly, "not when anyone is around."

Renee grabbed two mitten cookies and sat in the chair next to Claire. "Grab a cookie. In the middle of the table are the various icing bags and some decorative sprinkles."

"You have too much faith in me." Luke looked over the cookies, trying to decide which looked the easiest to decorate. The gingerbread cookies seemed straightforward — eyes, nose, and mouth, plus a few clothing details, all in one color. After washing his hands, Luke picked up a gingerbread boy and placed it in front of the remaining chair, the third being occupied by Claire's broken leg.

Picking up the white icing, he glanced at the sisters. Claire's brow furrowed with concentration, and Renee was biting her lower lip, tracing the outside of a mitten in red icing.

"You take this rather seriously," he said, sitting.

"Everything is serious with Renee," Claire said, teasing. "Haven't you figured that out yet?"

"I've seen the playful side of Renee," Luke countered.

"I'm sitting right here." Renee lifted her hands, and a squirt of icing shot out of her bag, landing on Claire's arm.

"Hey!" Claire yelled, reaching for a kitchen towel lying on the table. "I'll get you back for that."

"Please don't." Renee leaned back in her seat, eyes wide. "I don't have time to shower again before the parade. Why do we always pack too much into the last days before Christmas? Decorating cookies, the Santa parade, the talent show, it's going to be a long day." She glanced at the clock on the microwave, sighed, and went back to decorating.

"Do we know anyone who's performing in the talent show?" Luke asked.

"I don't," Renee said.

Claire tapped her chin. "I've heard several students talking about it, but I don't remember anyone specifically. Should be interesting."

Since she could sit and watch, Claire would be a judge for the talent show along with Mrs. White and Andy Hill.

Holly and Jolly would be there to pump up the crowd for each performer, and Alexis was the emcee for the event.

"Why don't we do this for the Eleven Pipers Piping event instead of caroling?" Renee asked. "See, we're piping." She held up a piping bag of icing. "And it would be warmer than walking around town in December."

"You're a wuss," Claire said. "People love carolers."

"Sure." Renee leaned over to create red ornaments on the Christmas tree cookie in front of her. "But the people who really want to do that and don't mind freezing their behinds off, can. Why make that the event for everyone?"

"Fair point," Luke said. "Should I put that on the feedback list?"

"Yes." Renee nodded. "Please mention it."

Her remark reminded him that she didn't intend to be here for the final committee meeting in two weeks.

Luke finished the first gingerbread boy. The bowtie was crooked, and one eye was bigger than the other, but overall he was pleasantly surprised with his decorating skill.

He just wished his skills at impressing women would work on Renee. He admired her focus and determination but wished she would take a breath and open herself up to living in the present moment, without running through a constant mental to-do list, assessing risks and improvement opportunities.

He wanted her to take joy in the moment, decorating cookies and being with family and friends. He hoped by now she would consider him a friend, with the possibility of more.

Chapter Nineteen

The talent show was winding down, and Renee was ready to drop after getting up early to bake cookies, hours of decorating, getting into costume, walking in the Santa parade, and now two and a half hours of the talent show.

They needed to limit the number of participants; opening it up to everyone and their mother, father, brother, and sister, was too much.

After three magic acts, four guitar solos, countless karaoke performances, and Heather Miller's twenty-four consecutive back bends, things were winding down. The last three acts were done—Sienna and Lila Watkins played ukuleles and sang "Somewhere Over the Rainbow", a group of four teenage drummers calling themselves the Four Green Hollies performed a lovely rendition of "Little Drummer Boy," and the Robert Hodge family sang, "Santa Claus is Coming to Town" in a rockin' version similar to Bruce Springsteen's—and the judges had their heads together, going over their notes.

As the judges conferred, Mr. Feno led the crowd in a holiday sing-along, starting with "Frosty the Snowman".

Renee and Luke were standing in front of the stage, still hamming it up for the crowd, when Renee noticed a TV cameraman and reporter approaching the judges' table. She looked at Luke, tilting her head towards the activity; he shrugged. *He must not have known they were coming either.*

Renee was mouthing the words as usual, watching Easton in the third row with his aunt, when she noticed Alexis approach Mr. Feno and speak in his ear.

After the song finished, Alexis stepped onto the stage and motioned for Renee and Luke to follow her.

Just as Renee turned to walk up the steps, she noticed the reporter approaching. She nearly tripped as she did a double take: it was Bryce Rhodes, the high school boyfriend who'd dumped her in front of everyone at prom.

No, no, no, this is not happening.

Grabbing onto the railing kept her from falling. *Thank goodness.*

As she stepped onto the stage, Bryce and the cameraman followed her. Bryce approached Alexis and said a few words that Renee could not hear. She had been between Luke and Alexis, but wanting to put as much distance between herself and Bryce as she could, she gently tugged on Luke's arm and moved past him.

Luke raised an eyebrow and whispered, "You okay?"

She nodded and smiled, trying to hide her rising panic.

Alexis spoke into the mic. "What a fun surprise, everyone! Bryce Rhodes from Channel Twenty-Seven is here to do a piece on our talent show!"

The crowd cheered. Renee clapped and smiled, smiled and clapped. *This is not about me. They will introduce the winners, and then we'll all go home. Maybe Bryce didn't even recognize me. No biggie.*

Once the crowd quieted, Alexis looked at Bryce for direction. He said a few words off the mic to the cameraman, and the cameraman moved to the other side of the stage.

Renee stiffened, fearing the cameraman was aiming at her. Then she realized he was pointed in that position to get the winners as they walked up onto the stage.

Bryce asked that they test using both microphones at the same time to make sure there wouldn't be feedback. That was successful, so Alexis stepped forward to announce the winners. Bryce stood back, letting the announcements play out without his commentary.

"All right, all right," Alexis began. "Let's hear it one more time for our amazing participants! Who knew Minier had such talent?"

She waited for the crowd to calm down. "On behalf of the judges, I want to announce our winners. In third place, Sienna and Lila Watkins!"

Renee clapped at the appropriate times and kept smiling through the other announcements, one cautious eye on Bryce. So far, he hadn't noticed her at all.

When the first-place winner was finally announced and received their trophy, Renee started to walk off the stage when she heard Bryce call her back. "Can the elves stay? They're a great backdrop!"

I'm a backdrop? Fine, better to be in the background than on camera. He must not know it's me. Even better.

She kept her head turned towards the other side of the gym, smiling and waving at the crowd, ignoring what Bryce and Alexis were doing.

The camera light turned on again, and Renee knew they were filming. *Five more minutes and I will be in my car on my way to Claire's. I think it's going to be a glass-of-wine kind of evening.*

Bryce's voice rang out. "Well, hello, Central Illinois. It's your old buddy, Bryce Rhodes, on the hunt for some small-town holiday cheer here in Minier, where they are just wrapping up their magical Twelve Holly Days of Christmas festivities with their annual talent show! I have here with me, Alexis Tooley-Owens, the Holiday Committee lead, and the winners of this year's contest.

"Alexis, will you please announce your winners for the viewers at home?"

Renee glanced over to see how Alexis was doing in front of the camera. She seemed poised and confident introducing each of the winners.

This has to be over soon; it sounds like he's live on air.

Once Alexis introduced the last winner, the audience cheered, but Bryce quickly cut them off. *Must not make great television. He probably wants to wrap up his segment.*

Bryce moved towards her end of the stage, the cameraman moving with him. *What the—*

Bryce stopped in front of her, speaking towards the camera. "Well, viewers, I've been told we are the last segment for today, and we have a few minutes before signing off. Why don't we end today's telecast with a little music to put us in the Christmas spirit?"

Turning towards Renee, he looked at her name tag and winked the eye farthest from the camera. "Well, Holly the Elf, why don't you lead us in a little sing-along? How about "We Wish You a Merry Christmas?""

Renee froze. Sing? On camera? Live on air? *This can not be happening to me!* She forgot the English language, forgot what words were, petrified by the camera with its blinking light pointing at her face. Her cheeks flushed, and she wanted to puke.

Bryce chuckled. "I think we got a—"

Renee glanced at Alexis. Had she set this up? Alexis' face was pale and her eyes wide. No, she was just as shocked as Renee.

Luke stepped between Renee and Bryce. "Holly hates to sing alone. Come on, everyone! We wish you a merry Christmas! We wish you a merry Christmas…"

The audience quickly jumped in, and Renee moved her lips to the words. She never stopped smiling, hoping her lip-syncing appeared legitimate.

As soon as the song ended, the camera swung to Bryce. "Happy holidays, everyone!" he shouted.

The camera light flipped off, and Renee rushed from the stage, Bryce's laughter ringing in her ears.

Evil jerk.

Passing the judges' table, Renee said to Claire, "Ask Luke to take you home. I'm—"

She didn't finish the thought. She was out the door.

Chapter Twenty

Renee grabbed a pair of black leggings and an over-sized cream-colored sweater. "What time are we going to Caleb's house?"

"Three," Claire mumbled. She was lying on the couch, reading a romantasy novel Renee didn't recognize.

"Great. I'm getting in the shower."

In the bathroom, she laid her clean clothes on the hamper and connected her phone to the speaker hanging in the shower. She was about to push play on her playlist when a loud knock startled her.

Waiting to hear whether Claire would ask her to answer the door, Renee leaned against the bathroom door to listen. She heard Claire get up from the couch and hobble towards the front door. When it opened, Renee heard Luke's voice and grimaced.

She'd stood him up for breakfast—she couldn't face him after yesterday's live broadcast debacle. Bryce's teasing had gone too far. Knowing that all of Central Illinois had witnessed her humiliation made her consider moving to Europe.

"Merry Christmas," Luke said.

Renee turned the shower on, hoping to avoid going out to the living room.

"Merry Christmas. I like the Santa hat, a nice change from the elf one," Claire said. "Come in. Want something to drink?"

"No, I can't stay. Is Renee in?"

"Shower."

"Oh. Okay. I wanted to drop off these presents for you. I'm taking my dad to my aunt's house for dinner, so I can't stay. Have a wonderful Christmas, Claire. My best to you, Renee, and your family."

"Open now?" Claire asked.

"No, save them for tomorrow."

The door opened and closed again. He was gone. Curiosity got the best of her, and she left the bathroom.

"Who was that?" she asked.

Claire was kneeling by the Christmas tree, her cast at an awkward angle, placing presents under it. She stood slowly, holding on to the TV stand, rolled her eyes, and looked Renee up and down. "You were listening. You know it was Luke."

"Ah, what did he bring? Muffins?"

"No, he brought gifts. They're under the tree, for tomorrow."

"Oh, that's nice. All right, getting in the shower now."

She should have talked to him; she could have given him her gift. Now, she would have to either rely on Claire to give it to him or drop it off at his place.

Yes, that would work. She'd drop it off before she left town on Tuesday.

Chapter Twenty-One

"Ready for another movie?" Luke asked his dad, getting up from the couch. He'd checked out several DVDs from the library. His dad refused to pay for cable or any streaming services. Luke had found it annoying in the beginning, but now he appreciated the simplicity and time for more reading.

He'd picked up the discarded wrapping paper and empty boxes after their Christmas morning gift exchange. They'd eaten their simple dinner of ham, mashed potatoes, glazed carrots, and yeast rolls, and were lounging around, relaxing.

"How about another piece of pie first?" Michael asked.

"For certain." Luke stacked their used plates and carried them into the kitchen. He refilled his coffee cup before slicing two more pieces of pumpkin pie. Grabbing the can out of the fridge, he covered each piece with dairy topping.

He wasn't attempting to make it pretty, just edible, but the effort of decorating the pie reminded him of cookie decorating with Renee and Claire.

Glancing at the small plate of cookies he'd brought home, he smiled at the memory of Renee teasing him. "Show him your work," she'd said.

He wondered how she was doing today. Was she over her embarrassment from the talent show or still reeling?

He hoped the joy of Christmas would help her to put the Bryce incident out of her mind.

Back in the living room, he handed his dad the pie. "Another movie or football?"

"Football. I think after this pie I'll take a little snooze. It won't bother me to miss part of a football game."

Luke sat in the recliner. "A nap sounds great." He wasn't concerned with football either, they had that in common.

Michael ate a bite of pie. "What's your plan for the week?"

"Besides your appointment Wednesday and catching up on some reading, I have nothing planned."

"No dates with that cute Renee?"

"No, I'm not sure when she's going back to Chicago. Things were hectic on Saturday, and she backed out of breakfast yesterday, so I don't know."

"Have you called her?"

"It's Christmas, and she's with her family."

Michael cut off another piece of his pie. "Well, you're doing the same thing, and you've got time to talk."

Luke finished his pie. His dad was right; he could call her now. If she didn't answer, she didn't answer.

He stood. "I'm going out to my apartment for a bit."

Michael chuckled. "Make that call, son."

Luke walked through the kitchen and out the back door. Sitting on the small porch was a wrapped Christmas gift. He leaned down and read the name tag. "To Luke from Renee."

Hmm, she didn't knock. Stealthy. Didn't she want to see me? Or maybe she didn't want to interrupt our holiday?

He picked up the gift and proceeded to his apartment.

He stared at his phone. Should he call her first and not mention the present, or call her to thank her for it?

The suspense got the better of him; he opened the gift.

Pulling the wrapping paper away, he found a gingerbread house kit. There was a note attached to it. "My favorite Christmas memories are of hours spent building these. I saw the picture of you and your mom making a gingerbread house. I hope this reminds you of those simpler days."

Luke's heart squeezed. He hadn't attempted a gingerbread house since he was nine; he wouldn't do this alone.

He picked up his phone and dialed her number. It rang several times and went to voicemail. He couldn't bring himself to leave a message. He wanted to talk to her in person. They had more to discuss than gingerbread houses.

Chapter Twenty-Two

Renee picked up her phone to check the time and smiled at the bracelet Luke had given her for Christmas. It was a Twelve Days of Christmas charm bracelet. Each charm represented one day in the song: five people dancing, drumming, or leaping, seven birds (two were two turtle doves), and a golden ring. It was so stinking cute and cheesy. She never wanted to take it off.

Glancing at the phone display, she saw she had just forty minutes until she'd need to leave to meet her friends at a New Year's Eve bash downtown. Her mood wasn't conducive to going out and partying until after midnight. Staying home and moping was even worse to contemplate, though.

The city had lost its sparkle since she'd come back. While at home, she'd felt like she had been reconnecting with her authentic self: a diligent (some would say over-achieving) middle child who loved her family, a photographer with a passion for seeing the world through her lens, only as close as she wanted to be, and someone who just might succumb to the magic of the holiday season and fall in love.

Her trendy but sterile apartment reminded her of work—her bathroom, where she would do her makeup and curl her hair before work; the closet with her pressed slacks, Ann Taylor suits, and crisp white blouses, just returned from the dry cleaners; the couch where she would sit and scroll through work emails on her phone; the round table in the kitchen where she would boot up her laptop and work for two or three hours after dinner.

She rarely had friends over, afraid that her apartment wouldn't be cool enough for her professional peers. She preferred to go out to meet people for drinks or dinner. While her apartment reminded her of work, it was also a place where she could retreat, close the door, turn on her favorite playlist, and rewind, away from the noise and bustle of city life.

It wouldn't be like that at home, that desire to cut herself off from the world. She could picture herself popping into Claire's place, unannounced, and having friends over to her own place for game nights, to watch a movie, or to have a cookout.

Suddenly, she longed for a small yard with a patio for a grill, a place for a fire pit, and comfortable lounge chairs.

Sighing, she turned on the curling iron and stared at herself in the mirror. Yesterday, her hairstylist had added fresh highlights to her hair and trimmed the ends. She had punched up her makeup for tonight with sparkly eyeshadow and a darker lipstick. Even if she didn't feel like going on the inside, the outside would be ready for the evening. *Fake it till you make it.*

That cliché reminded her of something Luke had said at their first Holly Days event. Something about being fake elves, but that was okay because the real ones were too busy this time of year to leave the North Pole.

She swallowed the lump in her throat that formed every time she thought about Luke. He'd called several times since she'd left Minier, but he never left a message. The thought of not seeing him every day was too painful, so she decided it was better to cut ties completely.

She let out another sigh and picked up her phone to turn up the volume on the music, but there was a loud rap on her door.

Surely the music isn't loud enough to annoy the neighbor.

She hit the pause button and went to the door. Talking before she even opened the door, she said, "Sorry, Mrs. Holmes, I'll turn it down."

To her surprise, it wasn't her sharp-eared neighbor standing in front of her. It was Luke, holding a gigantic bouquet of red and white roses.

"Luke? What? Doing?" she sputtered, self-consciously pulling her robe tight around her.

"Happy New Year's Eve," he said, shifting on his feet. He'd gotten a haircut since she'd seen him; the soft curls were gone. He wore a long black overcoat with a blue plaid scarf, black slacks, and shiny dress shoes.

"Are you going out? Hot date?" she asked. *What's he doing here on New Year's Eve?*

"Could I come in?" he asked, glancing over his shoulder at the door across from hers.

"Yes, sorry." She glanced down at her comfy pink fluffy bathrobe. "Give me a couple of minutes to get dressed?"

"Certainly."

"Have a seat." She pointed to the couch before closing her bedroom door.

She ignored the top and slacks she'd planned to wear out and opted for pink sweatpants and a purple, long-sleeved T-shirt. It was comfy; she could change again once Luke left.

Back in the living room, Luke was standing in his heavy coat, his back to her, in front of a series of framed photos she'd taken of various Chicago landmarks: Buckingham Fountain, the Chicago Picasso sculpture in Daley Plaza, the Chicago Theatre marquee sign, and the Cloud Gate sculpture, lovingly called "The Bean."

Hearing her, he turned. He was still holding the flower bouquet. "Are these your photographs?"

She nodded. "They are."

"Just incredible. You have a gift. Oh, these are for you," he said, holding out the bouquet. "They're from my dad and me. The dining table was an incredible surprise. He loves it. Caleb delivered it yesterday."

It was a beautiful oak table that her brother Caleb had made. She had bought it from him at a family discount. It had drained her savings, but it was so worth it. She smiled.

"I'm glad he loves it. You or he could have sent a thank-you note; you didn't have to drive almost three hours to bring me flowers on New Year's Eve. They're gorgeous! I'll get a vase."

"They're from the flower shop you told me about, In Bloom."

"How sweet! The flowers are gorgeous, and the ladies who work there are so wonderful."

She reached into a cabinet for a glass water pitcher that she occasionally used for flowers; no sense in keeping a vase in her tiny kitchen, as well.

"Yeah." Luke looked at her with narrowed eyes. "Your makeup's done. Are you going out? Hot date?" He repeated her words. A smile tugged at the corner of his mouth as he glanced at her very casual clothes.

"Going out with a group of friends. Not a date. A fancy bash we go to every year."

Why did I have to say fancy? Stupid.

"I came not just to thank you, but to talk to you. Haven't seen you since the talent show. I wanted to make sure you're recovered from that reporter's idiocy."

"Thanks. I think I'm recovered. Whenever it bothers me, I put it in perspective. In the grand scheme of things, when there are hungry, and lonely, and struggling people all over the world, embarrassment is nothing."

"That's a great perspective. But I'm still sorry it happened. I should have punched the guy on air."

Renee laughed at the thought of an elf punching a reporter live on air. "Oh. You didn't need to apologize. I own my freakout. Aren't you hot? You can take your coat off."

He looked down with a surprised expression that suggested he'd been unaware he was still wearing a coat. He shrugged it off, and laid it on the edge of the couch.

"No, you didn't freak out. He was an idiot, and you had every right to be offended. But that's not all I wanted to talk about. If you have the time, I have some things I'd like to say." He gestured to the couch.

She wanted to offer him something to drink. Isn't that what hosts were supposed to do? But even more, she wanted to hear what he had to say.

Needing a buffer, she picked up the small green velvet accent pillow, hugging it as she sat down sideways with one leg pulled up on the couch. Luke sat down on the middle cushion, close enough to touch, though neither of them did.

He sighed and seemed to gather his thoughts. "It was an eventful week," he said, turning to her, his green eyes more pronounced than usual because of his deep red sweater.

"You were off work. How eventful was it?"

"Dad had a scan on Wednesday. He's cancer-free."

"That's great news!"

"Yeah, I'm relieved."

"You could move back to Springfield. Get back into real estate."

"I suppose." He looked down and back at her, leaning slightly. "But I don't want to. This past year, caring for dad and getting involved in the community, Minier has been feeling like home. I don't want to leave."

"Oh." He wouldn't move here to Chicago, then.

"And I made a few inquiries about property in town. Still thinking about that bakery idea."

"Yeah?"

"I found something. You know the old bank that was a restaurant back in the day?"

"On Main Street, across from the beauty salon?"

"Yes, that's the one. It's up for sale. I thought I could buy it and turn it into a bakery. I wouldn't quit my job at the high school; I couldn't afford to. The bakery would be more of a passion hobby project. I could have a limited menu and just open for a couple of hours in the morning before school. Maybe open on Friday and Saturday nights as a dessert place rather than a full restaurant."

"That's an interesting concept. And I can see how the split hours might work with your job at the school. Are you going to do it?"

"I'm still thinking it through."

Renee squeezed the pillow to her chest and turned to put her back against the side of the couch, both feet on the cushion, fully facing Luke. "All right. I'm not sure what you need from me. I don't have any experience in the service industry. The only thing I might be able to help with are some design concepts, if you decide to go through with it. Maybe some photographs—"

Luke put his arm on the back of the couch and leaned towards her. "Photographs, of course. But I wanted to see what the chances are of you moving back to Minier."

"To be a partner in your business?" She shook her head. "I'm not a talented baker."

"Not to be a partner in a business, to be in a relationship with me. I know we only had the one official date, but..."

It was a date!

"We spent a lot of time together," he continued, "and you're incredibly smart, and funny, and beautiful. And I think you're searching for something too. Something real. Something more than a paycheck and a promotion."

Her breath caught. *Is that what I want? Something real with an amazing man like Luke?*

It sounded better than getting hit on by drunks at a New Year's Eve party.

"I don't know," she said. "Moving is a big decision, not a spur-of-the-moment one."

"You might want to make a slide presentation," he said, a smile threatening to spread across his handsome face. "I know you."

"Well, maybe."

A SWOT, or strengths, weaknesses, opportunities, and threats analysis, was not a bad idea. A list of pros and cons, at a minimum.

He stood and picked up his coat. "I'm kidding. Think about it. I know you're interviewing. Maybe the perfect position is about to land in your lap."

In this economy?

"Where are you going?" She stood and dropped the pillow on the floor, forgetting it was in her lap.

"Home."

"You're driving back now?"

"Yes, you said you were going out. I don't want to mess up your plans."

No way. I'm not going out now!

"I've decided to stay in tonight," she said. "Want to order takeout and watch the ball drop here?" She gestured towards the modest TV in the corner.

He raised an eyebrow. "Won't your friends miss you?"

"Probably not. I'll text and tell them I'm not coming."

"I don't want to drive home after midnight."

"You could stay."

He glanced at the couch. "Looks comfy."

"It's not bad." Not as comfortable as Claire's couch, but it was all right. "I've fallen asleep here a bunch of times."

"Any chance your brother's left some casual clothes here?" He looked down at his slacks and sweater.

"Definitely not. But I think we can come up with something. There are several stores within walking distance."

"It's New Year's Eve."

"Let's hurry." Renee slipped into sneakers. "I'm ready."

Luke shook his head, laughing. "Text your friends and let's go."

A few minutes before midnight, they gathered the remnants of their dinner: a medium pepperoni pizza, chicken fried rice, egg rolls, and a healthy serving of beef and broccoli. Not knowing how long delivery might take on this holiday evening, they'd ordered from two separate restaurants. The Chinese food arrived first, making nice appetizers before the pizza. They'd watched the ball drop in New York on the TV and were waiting for the Chicago countdown now.

They stood on Renee's small balcony with the sliding door slightly ajar so they could hear the countdown on the TV.

"Ready?" Renee asked.

"Always." Luke wore a Chicago Bulls tracksuit they'd found on a clearance rack in a sporting goods store. The red material made his green eyes pop even more than the elf suit had.

Fireworks would launch from Navy Pier out over Lake Michigan at midnight.

"Do you make resolutions?" Renee asked.

"I prefer goals." Luke put an arm around her and pulled her close. "Resolutions are too restrictive."

The warmth of his arm around her grounded her, and she took a deep breath, thankful to be here with Luke and not in a loud ballroom with three thousand revelers. "Restrictions are good. You know if you're doing it right."

Luke chuckled. "You would like resolutions, you goal-setter, you."

"Some habits are hard to break."

"Don't break any of your habits." Luke leaned down and kissed the side of her forehead. "They make you who you are. And I think you're perfect."

The sound of the countdown on the TV began, and cars on the street below began honking.

"Seven," Luke said.

"Six geese a-laying," Renee blurted, turning into his arms. He pulled her close and looked down into her eyes.

Luke chuckled. "Five golden rings."

They had to speak fast to keep up with the countdown.

"Four calling birds."

"Three French hens."

"Two turtle doves."

"One partridge!" they said in unison.

"Happy New Year, Holly," Luke whispered.

"Happy New Year, Jolly."

Luke grinned as he bent down, eyes on her lips. She froze momentarily, the anticipation almost too much.

When his lips touched hers, she wanted to squeal with excitement. Instead, she closed her eyes and basked in the sensation of being in this moment, with Luke, a man she would happily kiss every New Year's Eve for the rest of her life. She hoped she'd be able to show him how special he was in the new year. She resolved then and there to do just that.

Luke's lips were surprisingly warm and soft. He moved gently but with a touch of curiosity. When he pulled back from her, he smiled and pushed the hair back from her face.

"Hi," he said, glancing toward the lake and the fireworks. "That was a very special first kiss."

She shifted and put her head on his chest, looking toward the fireworks. "You don't get firework kisses every day."

"Firework kisses. I like that." He kissed the top of her head and held her close.

This was much better than a mistletoe kiss. The stars were twinkling above, fireworks split the sky with their grand colors, and she was here in Luke's arms, anticipating the year ahead and all the changes in store.

Epilogue

Two Months Later...

Renee hung the last of the photographs on the wall of Luke's bakery. A series of black and white photos of Minier landmarks, the grain towers, the water tower, the little free food pantry, a bench outside the library, and the roundabout with last year's Christmas tree standing in all its glory, adorned the walls.

Luke had suggested the photos, and Renee happily obliged.

"Last one?" Luke asked, stepping out of the back room. He carried a box with the stainless-steel napkin holders he'd purchased the day before at the restaurant-supply store in Peoria. Walking towards her, he set the box on a small table.

The room had six small tables with chairs, two antique display cases on either side of the counter, and a large window seat by the picture window. They'd painted the walls a deep taupe, which gave the room a rich, masculine feel. The trim was a warm vanilla color, which would be complimented by the warm, sweet aromas coming from the kitchen.

"Last one. What do you think?" Renee stood back, hands on hips, assessing the spacing between the frames.

"Perfect. Like you," he said, pulling her into a side hug.

"Oh, come on. We know that's not true." She was far from perfect, but she felt a thrill each time Luke gave her a compliment. "T minus one week. Everything seems to be right on schedule. How are you feeling?"

"Great. With you here, life's perfect." He held out his arms, and she stepped into them.

"I'm not sure about perfect, but a solid nine point nine."

Renee hadn't expected to feel this settled in her hometown so fast. An apartment in the same building as her sister's had become available on February first, so she'd moved off Claire's couch after another extended stay.

After countless interviews, she'd found a fully remote project-management position with a California company, which meant she could help Luke with the morning bakery rush. At least, they had high hopes there would be rushes once the bakery opened.

"Alexis called and said that everything is ready for the ribbon cutting next Friday," Renee said, thinking about the recent conversation with her past nemesis. After she moved home, they started a weekly coffee chat at Gary's diner. Alexis was encouraging Renee to consider running for mayor in the fall and volunteered to be her campaign manager.

Alexis's hands were full with her two part-time jobs and raising Easton on her own. Renee promised to be available for frequent babysitting sessions.

"That's great." Luke looked at his watch. "I have to run. Classes start in forty minutes. Walk you home?"

Renee laughed and glanced across the street to the front door of her building. "Go. I'll lock up. Dinner at my place tonight?"

He grimaced. "Mind if my dad tags along? I promised him I'd cook tonight."

"Of course not, the more the merrier. I'll text later with a dinner plan."

"Fantastic." Luke pulled her into an embrace.

Renee rested her head on his chest; the smell of his cologne calmed her nervous system. As much as she loved the woodsy smell, she preferred the smell of vanilla and sugar that clung to him on the weekends as he perfected the recipes he'd be using in the bakery.

Watching his joy as he baked made Renee consider her own passions. She no longer allowed work to consume her; she wasn't striving for a quick promotion or a bigger salary. She wanted more time with her family and friends, more time for photography, and loads more time with Luke.

He kissed her forehead before kissing her lips. "Love you, Ney," he said, before hugging her and walking towards the door.

She no longer minded the nickname.

"Love you!" Grabbing her keys, she shut off the lights and walked out the front door. Luke's car pulled away from the curb, and she waved.

Renee glanced up and down Main Street. A pickup truck rumbled to the stop sign on the corner before pulling into the intersection. Looking east towards the roundabout, she expected to see the first tulip blooms in a few days. Spring was coming, the season of new life in the gardens, the trees, and the fields.

She expected her love for Luke to continue to bloom and her roots in her hometown to deepen.

Not wanting to rush through life, she pushed thoughts of the holiday season with its Twelve Holly Days of Christmas aside. *The festival committee won't meet until April. It's too soon to start planning.*

Or was it? She laughed as she crossed the street.

WHAT'S NEXT?

Thank you for reading *Happy Holidates*! Please consider leaving an honest review on Amazon, Goodreads, Bookbub, or wherever you normally leave reviews.

Renee and Luke's story continues in the fun bonus epilogue. See where they are next Christmas. Get it here: https://dl.bookfunnel.com/h4vyjqlolu

If you enjoyed this story, check out the In Bloom series set in a flower shop in Central Illinois. Renee and her mom visited the store in *Happy Holidates*. You can jump into book 1, *Peonies for Paige*, on Amazon She's dreaming of the big city. He just wants to settle down. They've planted love, but can they tend it long enough to reap forever? You can find it here: https://mybook.to/10BURB5

ACKNOWLEDGMENTS

As always, I want to thank my husband, Tim, for supporting my writing dream. I love you!

A special shout out to my niece Kirsten to whom this book is dedicated. Early on, she helped me come up with Luke's name. We loved the biblical significance and the meaning "light-giving". I stole my niece's middle name for the main character, Renee.

A great big "thank you" to Sherri M, Chris B, Rick M, Patty B, and Paulette W for beta reading—thank you for your comments and attention to detail!

Thank you to the writing friends who encouraged me and held my feet to the fire: Lynn, Rebecca, Emily, Trish, Stephanie, Bryn, and so many others. I appreciate you and am always here to cheer you on!

Family is everything, and I want to thank my siblings, siblings-in-law, aunts, uncles, cousins, nieces, and nephews for all the encouragement. I love you infinity.

Thank you to the professionals who supported this project: Stephanie and Melissa at @Alt 19 Creative for the gorgeous cover, Rebecca H for Copyediting, and Stacy U for Proofreading! Thank you for putting up with my crazy last-minute requests and ridiculous deadlines.

And a heartfelt thank you to you, dear reader, for taking a chance on this story.

ABOUT THE AUTHOR

Kasey Kennedy is an Illinois gal through and through. She grew up in Central Illinois, finished college at Southern Illinois University Carbondale, and, soon afterward, moved to Chicago. She's been in Chicago or the surrounding suburbs ever since.

Kasey is happily married to her husband Tim and loves spending time with him—especially when that involves live music! If not attending a live show, they are usually listening to music, visiting family, watching movies, or planning their next trip.

When not dreaming up new characters and stories, Kasey is reading or planning what to read next. Occasionally, she pulls out the guitar that she has been trying to learn for 30+ years and strums enough to annoy her cat, Pepper.

Keep in touch. You can find me at:

FB – www.facebook.com/kaseykennedy8

IG – www.instagram.com/kaseykennedy8

Visit my website to sign up for my newsletter. Your email address will never be shared and you can unsubscribe any time you wish.

www.kasey-kennedy.com

I love hearing from readers! You can email me at kasey@kasey-kennedy.com